ALL LANI ARE COMPLETELY TRAINED TO CARE FOR THEIR EMPLOYERS.

"Good morning, doctor," a pleasant voice cut through Kennon's slumber.

Kennon looked around desperately for a moment. Then he saw her.

It was Copper, looking as beautiful and fresh and naked as ever.

"What are you doing here, young lady?" he asked angrily.

"I'm not a lady. Ladies are human. I'm a Lani. And I'm here to help you shower and dress, doctor."

This challenging novel by a new and exciting talent is a fascinating picture of a very possible world of a not impossible future....

THE LANI PEOPLE

J. F. BONE

BANTAM BOOKS / NEW YORK

THE LANI PEOPLE

A Bantam Book / published March 1962

All rights reserved.
© *Copyright, 1962, by Bantam Books, Inc.*
Published simultaneously in the
United States and Canada.

Bantam Books are published by Bantam Books, Inc. Its trade-mark, consisting of the words "Bantam Books" and the portrayal of a bantam, is registered in the United States Patent Office and in other countries. Marca Registrada. Printed in the United States of America. Bantam Books, Inc., 271 Madison Ave., New York 16, N. Y.

THE LANI PEOPLE

CHAPTER I

The boxed ad in the opportunities section of the *Kardon Journal of Allied Medical Sciences* stood out like a cut diamond in a handful of gravel. "Wanted," it read, "Veterinarian—for residency in active livestock operation. Single recent graduate preferred. Quarters and service furnished. Well-equipped hospital. Five-year contract, renewal option, starting salary 15,000 cr./annum with periodic increases. State age, school, marital status, and enclose recent tri-di with application. Address Box V-9, this journal."

Jac Kennon read the box a second time. There must be a catch to it. Nothing that paid a salary that large could possibly be on the level. Fifteen thousand a year was top pay even on Beta, and an offer like this for a new graduate was unheard of—unless Kardon was in the middle of an inflation. But Kardon wasn't. The planet's financial status was A-1. He knew. He'd checked that immediately after landing. Whatever might be wrong with Kardon, it wasn't her currency. The rate of exchange was 1.2–1 Betan.

A five-year contract—hmm—that would the seventy-five thousand. Figure three thousand a year for living expenses, that would leave sixty—plenty of capital to start a clinic. The banks couldn't turn him down if he had that much cash collateral.

Kennon chuckled wryly. He'd better get the job before he started spending the money he didn't have. He had 231 credits plus a few halves, tenths, and hundredths, a diploma in veterinary medicine, some textbooks, a few instruments, and a first-class spaceman's ticket. By watching his expenses he had enough money to live here for a month and if nothing came of his efforts to find a job on this planet, there was always his spaceman's ticket and another world.

Another world! There were over six thousand planets in the Brotherhood of Man. At two months per planet, not figuring transit time, it would take more than a thousand

Galactic Standard years to visit them all, and a man could look forward to scarcely more than five hundred at best. The habitat of Man had become too large. There wasn't time to explore every possibility.

But a man could have certain standards, and look until he found a position that fitted. The trouble was—if the standards were too high the jobs were too scarce. Despite the chronic shortage of veterinarians throughout the Brotherhood, there was a peculiar reluctance on the part of established practitioners to welcome recent graduates. Most of the ads in the professional journals read "State salary desired," which was nothing more than economic blackmail—a bald-faced attempt to get as much for as little as possible. Kennon grimaced wryly. He'd be damned if he'd sell his training for six thousand a year. Slave labor, that's what it was. There were a dozen ads like that in the *Journal*. Well, he'd give them a trial, but he'd ask eight thousand and full GEA benefits. Eight years of school and two more as an intern were worth at least that.

He pulled the portable voicewrite to a comfortable position in front of the view wall and began composing another of the series of letters that had begun months ago in time and parsecs away in space. His voice was a fluid counterpoint to the soft hum of the machine.

And as he dictated, his eyes took in the vista through the view wall. Albertsville was a nice town, too young for slums, too new for overpopulation. The white buildings were the color of winter butter in the warm yellow sunlight as the city drowsed in the noonday heat. It nestled snugly in the center of a bowl-shaped valley whose surrounding forest-clad hills gave mute confirmation to the fact that Kardon was still primitive, an unsettled world that had not yet reached the explosive stage of population growth that presaged maturity. But that was no disadvantage. In fact, Kennon liked it. Living could be fun on a planet like this.

It was abysmally crude compared to Beta, but the Brotherhood had opened Kardon less than five hundred years ago, and in such a short time one couldn't expect all the comforts of civilization. It required a high population density to supply them, and while Kardon was integrated its population was scarcely more than two hundred million. It would be some time yet before this world would achieve a Class I status. However, a Class II planet had some advantages. What it lacked in conveniences it made up in opportunities and elbow room.

A normal Betan would have despised this world, but Kennon wasn't normal, although to the casual eye he was a typical representative of the Medico-Technological Civilization, long legged, fair haired, and short bodied with the typical Betan squint that left his eyes mere slits behind thick lashes and heavy brows. The difference was internal rather than external.

Possibly it was due to the fact that his father was the commander of a Shortliner and most of his formative years had been spent in space. To Kennon, accustomed to the timeless horror of hyperspace, all planets were good, broad open places where a man could breathe unfiltered air and look for miles across distances unbroken by duralloy bulkheads and safety shields. On a planet there was spaciousness and freedom and after the claustrophobic confinement of a hypership any world was paradise. Kennon sighed, finished his letters, and placed them in the mail chute. Perhaps, this time, there would be a favorable reply.

CHAPTER II

Kennon was startled by the speed with which his letters were answered. Accustomed to the slower pace of Beta he had expected a week would elapse before the first reply, but within twenty-four hours nine of his twelve inquiries were returned. Five expressed the expected "Thank you but I feel that your asking salary is a bit high in view of your lack of experience." Three were frankly interested and requested a personal interview. And the last was *the* letter, outstanding in its quietly ostentatious folder—the reply from Box V-9.

Would Dr. Kennon call at 10 A.M. tomorrow at the offices of Outworld Enterprises Incorporated and bring this letter and suitable identifications? Kennon chuckled. Would he? There was no question about it. The address, 200 Central Avenue, was only a few blocks away. In fact, he could see the building from his window, a tall functional block of durilium and plastic, soaring above the others on the street, the sunlight gleaming off its clean square lines. He eyed it curiously, wondering what he would find inside.

The receptionist took his I.D. and the letter, scanned them

briefly, and slipped them into one of the message tubes beside her desk. "It will only be a moment, Doctor," she said impersonally. "Would you care to sit down?"

"Thank you," he said. The minute, reflected, could easily be an hour. But she was right. It was only a minute until the message tube clicked and popped a capsule onto the girl's desk. She opened it, and removed Kennon's I.D. and a small yellow plastic rectangle. Her eyes widened at the sight of the plastic card.

"Here you are, Doctor. Take shaft number one. Slip the card into the scanner slot and you'll be taken to the correct floor. The offices you want will be at the end of the corridor to the left. You'll find any other data you may need on the card in case you get lost." She looked at him with a curious mixture of surprise and respect as she handed him the contents of the message tube.

Kennon murmured an acknowledgment, took the card and his I.D., and entered the grav-shaft. There was the usual moment of heaviness as the shaft whisked him upward and deposited him in front of a thickly carpeted corridor.

Executive level, Kennon thought as he followed the receptionist's directions. No wonder she had looked respectful. But what was he doing here? The employment of a veterinarian wasn't important enough to demand the attention of a senior executive. The personnel section could handle the details of his application as well as not. He shrugged. Perhaps veterinarians were more important on Kardon. He didn't know a thing about this world's customs.

He opened the unmarked door at the end of the corridor, entered a small reception room, smiled uncertainly at the woman behind the desk, and received an answering smile in return.

"Come right in, Dr. Kennon. Mr. Alexander is waiting for you."

Alexander! The entrepreneur himself! Why? Numb with surprise Kennon watched the woman open the intercom on her desk.

"Sir, Dr. Kennon is here," she said.

"Bring him in," a smooth voice replied from the speaker.

Alexander X. M. Alexander, President of Outworld Enterprises—a lean, dark, wolfish man in his early sixties—eyed Kennon with a flat predatory intentness that was oddly disquieting. His stare combined the analytical inspection of the pathologist, the probing curiosity of the psychiatrist, and the weighing appraisal of the butcher. Kennon's thoughts about Alexander's youth vanished that instant. Those eyes belonged to a leader on the battlefield of galactic business.

Kennon felt the conditioned respect for authority surge through him in a smothering wave. Grimly he fought it down, knowing it was a sign of weakness that would do him no good in the interview which lay ahead.

"So you're Kennon," Alexander said. His lingua franca was clean and accentless. "I expected someone older."

"Frankly, sir, so did I," Kennon replied.

Alexander smiled, an oddly pleasant smile that transformed the hard straight lines in his face into friendly curves. "Business, Dr. Kennon, is not the sole property of age."

"Nor is a veterinary degree," Kennon replied.

"True. But one thinks of a Betan as someone ancient and sedate."

"Ours is an old planet—but we still have new generations."

"A fact most of us outsiders find hard to believe," Alexander said. "I picture your world as an ironclad society crystallized by age and custom into something rigid and inflexible."

"You would be wrong to do so," Kennon said. "Even though we are cultural introverts there is plenty of dynamism within our society."

"How is it that you happen to be out here on the edge of civilization?"

"I never said I was like my society," Kennon grinned. "Actually I suppose I'm one of the proverbial bad apples."

"There's more to it than that," Alexander said. "Your early years probably influenced you."

Kennon looked sharply at the entrepreneur. How much did the man really know about him? "I suppose so," he said indifferently.

Alexander looked pleased. "But even with your childhood experiences there must be an atavistic streak in you—a throwback to your adventurous Earth forebears who settled your world."

Kennon shrugged. "Perhaps you're right. I really don't know. Actually, I've never thought about it. It merely seemed to me that an undeveloped world offered more opportunity."

"It does," Alexander said. "But it also offers more work. If you're figuring that you can get along on the minimum physical effort required on the Central Worlds, you have a shock coming."

"I'm not that innocent," Kennon said. "But I am not so stupid that I can't apply modifications of Betan techniques to worlds as new as this."

Alexander chuckled. "I like you," he said suddenly. "Here

—read this and see if you'd care to work for me." He picked a contract form from one of the piles of paper on his desk and handed it to Kennon. "This is one of our standard work contracts. Take it back to your hotel and check it over. I'll expect to see you at this time tomorrow."

"Why waste time?" Kennon said. "The rapid-reading technique originated on Beta. I can tell you in fifteen minutes."

"Hmm. Certainly. Read it here if you wish. I like to get things settled—the sooner the better. Sit down, young man —and read. You can rouse me when you're finished." He turned his attention to the papers on his desk and within seconds was completely oblivious of Kennon, his face set in the rapt trancelike expression of a trained rapid reader.

Kennon watched for a moment as sheets of paper passed through Alexander's hands to be added to the pile at the opposite end of the desk. The man would do better, he thought, if he would have his staff transcribe the papers to microfilm that could be read through an interval-timed scanner. He might suggest that later. As for now, he shrugged and seated himself in the chair beside the desk. The quiet was broken only by the rustle of paper as the two rapt-faced men turned page after page with mechanical regularity.

Finally Kennon turned the last page, paused, blinked, and performed the necessary mental gymnastics to orient his time sense. Alexander, he noticed, was still engrossed, sunk in his autohypnotic trance. Kennon waited until he had finished the legal folder which he was reading and then gently intruded upon Alexander's concentration.

Alexander looked up blankly and then went through the same mental gyrations Kennon had performed a few minutes before. His eyes focused and became hard and alert.

"Well?" he asked. "What do you think of it?"

"I think it's the damnedest, trickiest, most unilateral piece of legalistics I've ever seen," Kennon said bluntly. "If that's the best you can offer, I wouldn't touch the job with a pair of forceps."

Alexander smiled. "I see you read the fine print," he said. There was quiet amusement in his voice. "So you don't like the contract?"

"No sensible man would. I'm damned if I'll sign commitment papers just to get a job. No wonder you're having trouble getting professional help. If your contracts are all like that it's a wonder anyone works for you."

"We have no complaints from our employees," Alexander said stiffly.

"How could you? If they signed that contract you'd have a perfect right to muzzle them."

"There are other applicants for this post," Alexander said.

"Then get one of them. I wouldn't be interested."

"A spaceman's ticket is a good thing to have," Alexander said idly. "It's a useful ace in the hole. Besides, you have had three other job offers—all of which are good even though they don't pay fifteen Ems a year."

Kennon did a quick double take. Alexander's investigative staff was better than good. It was uncanny.

"But seriously, Dr. Kennon, I am pleased that you do not like that contract. Frankly, I wouldn't consider employing you if you did."

"Sir?"

"That contract is a screen. It weeds out the careless, the fools, and the unfit in one operation. A man who would sign a thing like that has no place in my organization." Alexander chuckled at Kennon's blank expression. "I see you have had no experience with screening contracts."

"I haven't," Kennon admitted. "On Beta the tests are formal. The Medico-Psych Division supervises them."

"Different worlds, different methods," Alexander observed. "But they're all directed toward the same goal. Here we aren't so civilized. We depend more on personal judgment." He took another contract from one of the drawers of his desk. "Take a look at this. I think you'll be more satisfied."

"If you don't mind I'll read it now," Kennon said.

Alexander nodded.

"It's fair enough," Kennon said, "except for Article Twelve."

"The personal privilege section?"

"Yes."

"Well, that's the contract. You can take it or leave it."

"I'll leave it," Kennon said. "Thank you for your time." He rose to his feet, smiled at Alexander, and turned to the door. "Don't bother to call your receptionist," he said. "I can find my way out."

"Just a minute, Doctor," Alexander said. He was standing behind the desk, holding out his hand.

"Another test?" Kennon required.

Alexander nodded. "The critical one," he said. "Do you want the job?"

"Of course."

"Without knowing more about it?"

"The contract is adequate. It defines my duties."

7

"And you think you can handle them?"

"I know I can."

"I notice," Alexander observed, "that you didn't object to other provisions."

"No, sir. They're pretty rigid, but for the salary you are paying I figure you should have some rights. Certainly you have the right to protect your interests. But that Article Twelve is a direct violation of everything a human being should hold sacred besides being a violation of the Peeper Laws. I'd never sign a contract that didn't carry a full Peeper rider."

"That's quite a bit."

"That's the minimum," Kennon corrected. "Naturally, I won't object to mnemonic erasure of matters pertaining to your business once my contract's completed and I leave your employment. But until then there will be no conditioning, no erasures, no taps, no snoopers, and no checkups other than the regular periodic psychans. I'll consult with you on vacation time and will arrange it to suit your convenience. I'll even agree to emergency recall, but that's the limit." Kennon's voice was flat.

"You realize I'm agreeing to give you a great deal of personal liberty," Alexander said. "How can I protect myself?"

"I'll sign a contingency rider," Kennon said, "if you will specify precisely what security matters I am not to reveal."

"I accept," Alexander said. "Consider yourself hired." He touched a button on his desk. "Prepare a standard 2-A contract for Dr. Jac Kennon's signature. And attach two riders, a full P-P—yes, no exceptions—and a security-leak contingency, Form 287-C. Yes—that's right—that one. And strike out all provisions of Article Twelve which conflict with the Peeper Laws. —Yes. Now—and finish it as soon as you can." He touched another button. "Well, that's that," he said. "I hope you'll enjoy being a member of our group."

"I think I shall," Kennon said. "You know, sir, I would have waived part of that last demand if you had cared to argue."

"I know it," Alexander said. "But what concessions I could have wrung from you would be relatively unimportant beside the fact that you would be unhappy about them later. What little I could have won here, I'd lose elsewhere. And since I want you, I'd prefer to have you satisfied."

"I see," Kennon said. Actually he didn't see at all. He looked curiously at the entrepreneur. Alexander *couldn't* be as easy as he seemed. Objectivity and dispassionate weighing and balancing were nice traits and very helpful ones, but in the bear pit of galactic business they wouldn't keep their owner alive for five minutes. The interworld trade sharks would have skinned him long ago and divided the stripped carcass of his company between them.

But Outworld was a "respected" company. The exchange reports said so—which made Alexander a different breed of cat entirely. Still, his surface was perfect—polished and impenetrable as a duralloy turret on one of the latest Brotherhood battleships. Kennon regretted he wasn't a sensitive. It would be nice to know what Alexander really was.

"Tell me, sir," Kennon asked. "What are the real reasons that make you think I'm the man you want?"

"And you're the young man who's so insistent on a personal privacy rider," Alexander chuckled. "However, there's no harm telling you. There are several reasons.

"You're from a culture whose name is a byword for moral integrity. That makes you a good risk so far as your ethics are concerned. In addition you're the product of one of the finest educational systems in the galaxy—and you have proven your intelligence to my satisfaction. You also showed me that you weren't a spineless 'yes man.' And finally, you have a spirit of adventure. Not one in a million of your people would do what you have done. What more could an entrepreneur ask of a prospective employee?"

Kennon sighed and gave up. Alexander wasn't going to reveal a thing.

"All I hope," Alexander continued affably, "is that you'll find Outworld Enterprises as attractive as did your predecessor Dr. Williamson. He was with us until he died last month—better than a hundred years."

"Died rather young, didn't he?"

"Not exactly, he was nearly four hundred when he joined us. My grandfather was essentially conservative. He liked older men, and Old Doc was one of his choices—a good one, too. He was worth every credit we paid him."

"I'll try to do as well," Kennon said, "but I'd like to warn you that I have no intention of staying as long as he did. I want to build a clinic and I figure sixty thousand is about enough to get started."

"When will you veterinarians ever learn to be organization men?" Alexander asked. "You're as independent as tomcats."

Kennon grinned. "It's a breed characteristic, I guess."

Alexander shrugged. "Perhaps you'll change your mind after you've worked for us."

"Possibly, but I doubt it."

"Tell me that five years from now," Alexander said—"Ah—here are the contracts." He smiled at the trim secretary who entered the room carrying a stack of papers.

"The riders are as you asked, sir," the girl said.

"Good. Now, Doctor, if you please."

"You don't mind if I check them?" Kennon asked.

"Not at all. And when you're through, just leave them on the desk—except for your copy, of course." Alexander scrawled his signature on the bottom of each contract. "Don't disturb me. I'll be in contact with you. Leave your whereabouts with your hotel." He turned to the papers in front of him, and then looked up for the last time. "Just one more thing," he said. "You impress me as a cautious man. It would be just as well if you carried your caution with you when you leave this room."

Kennon nodded, and Alexander turned back to his work.

CHAPTER III

"I'd never have guessed yesterday that I'd be here today," Kennon said as he looked down at the yellow waters of the Xantline Sea flashing to the rear of the airboat at a steady thousand kilometers per hour as they sped westward in the middle traffic level. The water, some ten thousand meters below, had been completely empty for hours as the craft hurtled through the equatorial air.

"We have to move fast to stay ahead of our ulcers," Alexander said with a wry smile. "Besides, I wanted to get away from the Albertsville offices for awhile."

"Three hours' notice," Kennon said. "That's almost too fast."

"You had nothing to keep you in the city, and neither did I—at least nothing important. There are plenty of females where we are going and I need you on Flora—not in Albertsville. Besides I can get you there faster than if you waited for a company transport."

"Judging from those empty sea lanes below, Flora must be an out-of-the-way place," Kennon said.

"It is. It's out of the trade lanes. Most of the commercial traffic is in the southern hemisphere. The northern hemisphere is practically all water. Except for Flora and the Otpens there isn't a land area for nearly three thousand kilometers in any direction, and since the company owns Flora and the surrounding island groups there's no reason for shipping to come there. We have our own supply vessels, a Discovery Charter, and a desire for privacy. —Ah! It won't be long now. There's the Otpens!" Alexander pointed at a smudge on the horizon that quickly resolved into an irregular chain of tiny islets that slipped below them. Kennon got a glimpse of gray concrete on one of the larger islands, a smudge of green trees, and white beaches against which the yellow waters dashed in smothers of foam.

"Rugged-looking place," he murmured.

"Most of them are deserted. Two support search and warning stations and automatic interceptors to protect our property. Look!—there's Flora." Alexander gestured at the land mass that appeared below.

Flora was a great green oval two hundred kilometers long and about a hundred wide.

"Pretty, isn't it?" Alexander said as they sped over the low range of hills and the single gaunt volcano filling the eastward end of the island and swept over a broad green valley dotted with fields and orchards interspersed at intervals by red-roofed structures whose purpose was obvious.

"Our farms," Alexander said redundantly. The airboat crossed a fair-sized river. "That's the Styx," Alexander said. "Grandfather named it. He was a classicist in his way—spent a lot of his time reading books most people never heard of. Things like the *Iliad* and *Gone with the Wind*. The mountains he called the Apennines, and that volcano's Mount Olympus. The marshland to the north is called the Pontine Marshes—our main road is the Camino Real." Alexander grinned. "There's a lot of Earth on Flora. You'll find it in every name. Grandfather was an Earthman and he used to get nostalgic for the homeworld. Well—there's Alexandria coming up. We've just about reached the end of the line."

Kennon stared down at the huge gray-green citadel resting on a small hill in the center of an open plain. It was a Class II Fortalice built on the efficient star-shaped plan of half a millennium ago—an ugly spiky pile of durilium, squat and massive with defensive shields and weapons which could still withstand hours of assault by the most modern forces.

"Why did he build a thing like that?" Kennon asked.

"Alexandria?—well, we had trouble with the natives when we first came, and Grandfather had a synthesizer and tapes for a Fortalice in his ship. So he built it. It serves the dual purpose of base and house. It's mostly house now, but it's still capable of being defended."

"And those outbuildings?"

"They're part of your job."

The airboat braked sharply and settled with a smooth, sickeningly swift rush that left Kennon gasping—feeling that his stomach was still floating above him in the middle level. He never had become accustomed to an airboat's landing charateristics—spacers were slower and steadier. The ship landed gently on a pitted concrete slab near the massive radiation shields of the barbicaned entranceway to the fortress. Projectors in polished durralloy turrets swiveled to point their ugly noses at them. It gave Kennon a queasy feeling. He never liked to trust his future to automatic machinery. If the analyzers failed to decode the ship's I.D. properly, Kennon, Alexander, the ship, and a fair slice of surrounding territory would become an incandescent mass of dissociated atoms.

"Grandfather was a good builder," Alexander said proudly. "Those projectors have been mounted nearly four hundred years and they're still as good as the day they were installed."

"I can see that," Kennon said uncomfortably. "You ought to dismantle them. They're enough to give a man the weebies."

Alexander chuckled. "Oh—they're safe. The firing mechanism's safetied. But we keep them in operating condition. You never can tell when they'll come in handy."

"I knew Kardon was primitive, but I didn't think it was that bad. What's the trouble?"

"None—right now," Alexander said obliquely, "and since we've shown we can handle ourselves there probably won't be any more."

"You must raise some pretty valuable stock if the competition tried to rustle them in the face of that armament."

"We do." Alexander said. "Now if you'll follow me"—the entrepreneur opened the cabin door letting in a blast of heat and a flood of yellow sunlight.

"Great Arthur Fleming!" Kennon exploded. "This place is a furnace!"

"It's hot out here on the strip," Alexander admitted, "but its cool enough inside. Besides, you'll get used to this quickly enough—and the nights are wonderful. The evening rains cool things off. Well—come along." He began walking toward the arched entrance to the great building some hundred meters away. Kennon followed looking around curiously. So this was to be his home for the next five years? It didn't look particularly inviting. There was a forbidding air about the place that was in stark contrast to its pleasant surroundings.

They were only a few meters from the archway when a stir of movement came from its shadow—the first life Kennon had seen since they descended from the ship. In this furnace heat even the air was quiet. Two women came out of the darkness, moving with quiet graceful steps across the blistering hot concrete. They were naked except for a loincloth, halter, and sandals and so nearly identical in form and feature that Kennon took them to be twins. Their skins were burned a deep brown that glistened in the yellow sunlight.

Kennon shrugged. It was none of his business how his employer ran his household or what his servants wore or didn't wear. Santos was a planet of nudists, and certainly this hot sun was fully as brilliant as the one which warmed that tropical planet. In fact, he could see some virtue in wearing as little as possible. Already he was perspiring.

The two women walked past them toward the airboat. Kennon turned to look at them and noticed with surprise that they weren't human. The long tails curled below their spinal bases were adequate denials of human ancestry.

"Humanoids!" he gasped. "For a moment I thought——"

"Gave you a start—eh?" Alexander chuckled. "It always does when a stranger sees a Lani for the first time. Well—now you've seen some of the livestock what do you think of them?"

"I think you should have hired a medic."

Alexander shook his head. "No—it wouldn't be reasonable or legal. You're the man for the job."

"But I've no experience with humanoid types. We didn't cover that phase in our studies—and from their appearance they'd qualify as humans anywhere if it weren't for those tails!"

"They're far more similar than you think," Alexander said. "It just goes to show what parallel evolution can do. But there are differences."

"I never knew that there was indigenous humanoid life on Kardon," Kennon continued. "The manual says nothing about it."

"Naturally. They're indigenous only to this area."

"That's impossible. Species as highly organized as that simply don't originate on isolated islands."

"This was a subcontinent once," Alexander said. "Most

of it has been inundated. Less than a quarter of a million years ago there was over a hundred times the land area in this region than exists today. Then the ocean rose. Now all that's left is he midcontinent plateau and a few mountaintops. You noted, I suppose, that this is mature topography except for that range of hills to the east. The whole land area at the time of flooding was virtually a peneplain. A rise of a few hundred feet in the ocean level was all that was needed to drown most of the land."

"I see. Yes, it's possible that life could have developed here under those conditions. A peneplain topography argues permanence for hundreds of millions of years."

"You have studied geology?" Alexander asked curiously.

"Only as part of my cultural base," Kennon said. "Merely a casual acquaintance."

"We think the Lani were survivors of that catastrophe— and with their primitive culture they were unable to reach the other land masses," Alexander shrugged. "At any rate they never established themselves anywhere else."

"How did you happen to come here?"

"I was born here," Alexander said. "My grandfather discovered this world better than four hundred years ago. He picked this area because it all could be comfortably included in Discovery Rights. It wasn't until years afterward that he realized the ecological peculiarities of this region."

"He certainly capitalized on them."

"There was plenty of opportunity. The plants and animals here are different from others in this world. Like Australia in reverse."

Kennon looked blank, and Alexander chuckled. "Australia was a subcontinent on Earth," he explained. "Its ecology, however, was exceedingly primitive when compared with the rest of the planet. Flora's on the contrary, was—and is—exceedingly advanced when compared with other native life forms on Kardon."

"Your grandfather stumbled on a real bonanza," Kennon said.

"For which I'm grateful," Alexander grinned. "It's made me the biggest operator in this sector of the galaxy. For practical purposes I own an independent nation. There's about a thousand humans here, and nearly six thousand Lani. We're increasing the Lani now, since we found they have commercial possibilities. Up to thirty years ago we merely used them for labor."

Kennon didn't speculate on what Alexander meant. He

knew. For practical purposes, his employer was a slave trader—or would have been if the natives were human. As it was, the analogy was so close that it wasn't funny.

They entered the fortress, passed through a decontamination chamber that would have done credit to an exploration ship, and emerged dressed in tunics and sandals that were far more appropriate and comfortable in this tropical climate.

"That's one of Old Doc's ideas," Alexander said gesturing at the door from which they had emerged. "He was a hound for sanitation and he infected us with the habit." He turned and led the way down an arched corridor that opened into a huge circular room studded with iris doors.

Kennon sucked his breath in with a low gasp of amazement. The room was a gem of exquisite beauty. The parquet floor was inlaid with rare hardwoods from a hundred different worlds. Parthian marble veneer covered with lacy Varl tapestries from Santos formed the walls. Delicate ceramics, sculpture, and bronzes reflected the art of a score of different civilizations. A circular pool, festooned with lacelike Halsite ferns, stood in the center of the room, surrounding a polished black granite pedestal on which stood an exquisite bronze of four Lani females industriously and eternally pouring golden water from vases held in their shapely hands. "Beautiful," Kennon said softly.

"We like it," Alexander said.

"We?"

"Oh yes—I forgot to tell you about the Family," Alexander said grimly. "I run Outworld, and own fifty per cent of it. The Family owns the other fifty. There are eight of them—the finest collection of parasites in the entire galaxy. At the moment they can't block me since I also control my cousin Douglas's shares. But when Douglas comes of age they will be troublesome. Therefore I defer to them. I don't want to build a united opposition. Usually I can get one or more of them to vote with me on critical deals, but I always have to pay for their support." Alexander's voice was bitter as he touched the dilate button on the iris door beside him. "You'll have to meet them tonight. There's five of them here now."

"That isn't in the contract," Kennon said. He was appalled at Alexander. Civilized people didn't speak of others that way, even to intimates.

"It can't be helped. You must meet them. It's part of the job." Alexander's voice was grim. "Mother, Cousin Anne,

Douglas, and Eloise like to play lord of the manor. Cousin Harold doesn't care—for which you should be grateful."

The door dilated, and Alexander ushered Kennon into the room. The Lani sitting on the couch opposite the door leaped to her feet, her mouth opening in an O of surprise. Her soft snow-white hair, creamy skin, and bright chinablue eyes were a startling contrast to her black loincloth and halter. Kennon stared appreciatively.

Her effect on Alexander, however, was entirely different. His face darkened. "You!" he snapped. "What are you doing here?"

"Serving, sir," the Lani said.

"On whose authority?"

"Man Douglas, sir."

Alexander groaned. "You see," he said, turning to Kennon. "We need someone here with a little sense. Like I was telling you, the Family'd"—he stopped abruptly and turned back to the Lani. "Your name and pedigree," he demanded.

"Silver Dawn, sir—out of White Magic—platinum experimental type—strain four."

"I thought so. How long have you been inhouse?"

"Almost a month, sir."

"You're terminated. Report to Goldie and tell her that Man Alexander wants you sent back to your group."

The Lani's eyes widened. "Man Alexander!—You?"

Alexander nodded.

"Gosh!" she breathed. "The big boss!"

"Get moving," Alexander snapped, "and tell Goldie to report to me in my quarters."

"Yes, sir, right away, sir!" The Lani ran, disappearing through the door they had entered with a flash of shapely white limbs.

"That Douglas!" Alexander growled. "Leave that young fool alone here for six months and he'd disrupt the entire operation. The nerve of that young pup—requisitioning an experimental type for household labor. Just what does he think he's doing?"

The question obviously didn't demand a reply, so Kennon kept discreetly silent as Alexander crossed the room to the two doors flanking the couch on which the Lani had sat. He opened the left-hand one revealing a modern grav-shaft that carried them swiftly to the uppermost level. They walked down a short corridor and stopped before another door. It opened into a suite furnished with stark functional simplicity. It fitted the entrepreneur's outward personality so exactly that Kennon had no doubt that this was Alexander's quarters.

"Sit down, Kennon. Relax while you can," Alexander said as he dropped into a chair and crossed his sandaled feet. "I'm sure you have many questions, but they can wait. You might as well get some rest. You'll have little enough later. The Family will probably put you through the meat grinder, but remember that they don't control this business. You're my man."

Kennon had hardly seated himself in another chair when the door opened and a plump pink-skinned Lani entered. She was considerably older than the silver-haired one he had seen earlier, and her round face was smiling.

"Ah, Goldie," Alexander said. "I understand Man Douglas has been giving you quite a time."

"It's high time you came back, sir," she said. "Since Old Doc died, Man Douglas has been impossible. He's been culling the staff and replacing them with empty-headed fillies whose only claim to usefulness is that they can fill out a halter. Pretty soon this place will be a pigsty."

"I'll take care of that," Alexander promised. "Now I'd like you to meet Old Doc's replacement. This is Dr. Kennon, our new veterinarian."

"Pleased, I'm sure," Goldie said. "You look like a nice man."

"He is," Alexander said, "but he's just as hard as Old Doc—and he'll have the same powers. Goldie's the head housekeeper," Alexander added. "She's an expert, and you'd do well to take her advice on assignments."

Kennon nodded.

"Have a maid bring us a light meal and something to drink," Alexander said. "Have a couple of porters take Dr. Kennon's things to Old Doc's house. Find Man Douglas and tell him I want to see him at once. Tell the Family that I've arrived and will see them in the Main Lounge at eight tonight. Tell Blalok I'll be seeing him at nine. That's all."

"Yes sir," Goldie said and left the room, her tail curling buoyantly.

"A good Lani," Alexander commented. "One of the best. Loyal, trustworthy, intelligent. She's been running Alexandria for the past ten years, and should be good for at least ten more."

"Ten?—how old is she."

"Thirty."

"Thirty—*years?*"

17

Alexander nodded.

"Good Lord Lister! I'd have guessed her at least three hundred!"

"Wrong life scale. Lani only live about one tenth as long as we do. They're mature at twelve and dead at fifty." Alexander sighed. "That's another difference. Even without agerone we'd live to be a hundred."

"Have you tried gerontological injections?"

"Once. They produced death in about two days. Killed five Lani with them." Alexander's face darkened at an unpleasant memory. "So we don't try any more," he said. "There are too many differences." He stretched. "I'd tell you more about them but it'll be better to hear it from Evald Blalok. He's our superintendent. Steve Jordan can tell you a lot, too. He runs the Lani Division. But right now let's wait for Cousin Douglas. The pup will take his time about coming—but he'll do it in the end. He's afraid not to."

"I'd rather not," Kennon said. "It's poor manners to be injected into a family affair—especially when I'm just one of the employees."

"You're *not* just one of the employees. You are the Station Veterinarian, and as such you hold an authority second only to Blalok and myself. You and Blalok are my hands, ears, and eyes on Flora. You are responsible to me—and to me alone. While I defer at times to the desires of the Family, I do not have to. I run Outworld Enterprises and all the extensions of that organization. I possess control —and the Family knows it. My men are respected and furthermore they know everything that goes on." He smiled icily. "In a way it's quite a healthy situation. It keeps my relatives under control. Somehow they dislike being disciplined before outsiders. Now think no more about it." Alexander stood up and walked over to one of the windows opening onto the broad roof gardens, and stood looking at the sun-drenched greenery.

"Odd, isn't it," Alexander said, "how beautiful nature is and how simple things are in a state of nature. It's only when man interjects himself onto a scene that things get complicated. Take Flora for instance. Before Grandfather came here, it must have been a pleasant place with the simple natives happy in their paradise. But that's all changed now. We have taken over—and they, like other lesser creatures on other worlds, have been bent to our will and uses. I could pity them, but being human I cannot afford that luxury."

Kennon understood. He, too, had felt that sensation, that

odd tightening of the throat when he first saw a Varl on Santos. The Varl had been the dominant life form there until men had come. Now they were just another animal added to humanity's growing list of pets and livestock. The little Varl with their soft-furred bodies and clever six-fingered hands made excellent pets and precision workmen. The products of those clever hands, the tiny instruments, the delicate microminiaturized control circuits, the incredibly fine lacework and tapestries, formed the bulk of Santos' interstellar trade.

He had owned a Varl once and had delighted in its almost human intelligence. But the Varl weren't human and there lay their tragedy. Two thousand years of human dominaton had left them completely dependent on their conquerors. They were merely intelligent animals—and that was all they would ever be until the human race changed its cultural pattern or was overthrown. The one alternative was as unlikely as the other. Humanity had met some fierce competitors, but none with its explosive acquisitive nature, and none with its drive to conquer, colonize, and rule. And probably it never would.

The little Varl were one race among hundreds that had fallen before the fierceness and the greed of men. But unlike most others, the Varl were not combative. Therefore they had survived.

Yet had it been necessary to reduce them to slavery? They would never be a threat. Not only were they essentially gentle and noncombative, but their delicate bodies could not stand the strains of spaceflight. They were trapped on their world. Why should they be forced into so subordinate a role?—Why was humanity so jealous of its dominance that no other species could exist except by sufferance? Why after five thousand years of exploration, invasion, and colonization did the human race still consider the galaxy as its oyster, and themselves uniquely qualified to hold the knife? He hadn't thought this way since he had given the Varl to his girl friend of the moment, and had blasted off for Beta. Now the questions returned to haunt him. As a Betan, the haunting was even more acute, since Beta had a related problem that was already troublesome and would become more acute as the years passed.

He shrugged and laid the thought aside as a slim, dark-haired Lani entered pushing a service cart ahead of her. The two men ate silently, each busy with his own thoughts. And behind the view wall of Alexander's apartment Kardon's brilliant yellow sun sank slowly toward the horizon, filling the sky with flaming colors of red and gold, rimmed by the blues and purples of approaching night. The sunset was gaudy and blatant, Kennon thought with mild distaste, unlike the restful day-end displays of his homeworld.

CHAPTER IV

Douglas Alexander was a puffy-faced youngster with small intolerant eyes set in folds of fat above a button nose and a loose-lipped sensual mouth. There was an odd expression of defiance overlaid with fear on his pudgy features. Looking at him, Kennon was reminded of a frightened dog, ready either to bite or cower.

But it wasn't Douglas who held his eye. It was the two Lani who followed him into the room. Every line of their bodies was perfection that spoke volumes about generations of breeding for physical elegance. They moved with a co-ordinated grace that made Douglas look even more clumsy by contrast. And they were identical, twin cream-and-gold works of art. They were completely nude—and Kennon for the first time in his life fully appreciated the beauty of an unclad female. To cover them would be sacrilege, and ornaments would only detract from their exquisite perfection.

Kennon knew that he was staring like an idiot. Alexander's amused smile told him that much. With an effort he composed his startled features.

The pair looked at him with soft violet eyes—and it was as though some psychic bathhouse attendant had poured ice water down his spine. For he had seen that look before, that liquid introspective look in the velvet eyes of cattle. He shivered. For a moment he had been thinking of them as human. And somehow the lack of that indefinable something called humanity robbed them of much of their glamour. They were still beautiful, but their beauty had become impersonal.

"Don't take these as representative of the Lani," Alexander said suddenly. "They're a special case, a very special case." He glared at his cousin. "Damn your impudence," he said without heat. "I sent for you—not your toys. Send them away."

Douglas sulkily thrust out his lower lip. "You can't talk to me like that, Cousin Alex," he began. "I'm just as——"

"You heard me, Douglas. *Out!*" Alexander's voice didn't rise but it cut like a whip.

"Oh, very well," Douglas said. "I can't fight you—yet." He turned to the humanoids. "You heard the Boss-man. Go home."

The two nodded in unison and departed quickly. Somehow Kennon got the impression that they were happy to leave.

"Just wait," Douglas said. "You can't boss me forever. Just wait. I'll reach my majority in five years. I can vote my shares then—and then I'll fix you. You won't be so high and mighty then, Mr. Big. I'll throw in with the rest of the Family. They don't like you too much."

"Don't hold your breath waiting for the Family to help you," Alexander said. "They wouldn't have anyone else *but* me handle the finances. They love money too much. And until you get your inheritance remember one thing—I'm master here."

"I know it," Douglas said, and then curiously—"who's the oddball?" He gestured at Kennon with a pudgy thumb.

"Our new veterinarian, Dr. Kennon."

"Oh—great! Now you tell me!"

"There's nothing like making a good first impression," Alexander said with ironic emphasis. "I hope he cuts you off from the Lani. He'll have the authority to do it, since he's taking Old Doc's place."

"He can't. I'm an owner. I own——"

"You own nothing. You're a minor. And under the terms of Grandfather's will, you'll own nothing except an allowance until you reach legal age. And that brings me to the reason I brought you here. Just when did you gain the right to reorganize the household staff? Just when did you get the power to interfere with the experimental program?"

Douglas flushed dull red and bit his lip. "Do we have to go into this in front of strangers?"

"Kennon's my agent," Alexander said coldly, "and he might as well learn about you and the others from the start."

"Well—what do you want him to do—watch me crawl?" Douglas asked bitterly. "You'll make me do it. You always do. Do you want me to beg, to say I was wrong, to promise I won't do it again?"

"You've done that already," Alexander said. "Several times. You need a lesson. I won't have you meddling with valuable animals."

"And what are you going to do about it?"

"Put you where you can do no more damage. As of tomorrow you'll go to Otpen One."

Douglas paled. His lips quivered, and his eyes flicked uneasily as he watched Alexander's granite face. "You don't mean that," he said finally. "You're joking."

"I never joke about business."

"But you can't do that! I'll tell the Family. They won't let you."

"I already have their consent," Alexander said. "I obtained it after your last escapade. You'll be happy out there. You can play tin god all you like. Master of life and death on a two-acre island. No one will mind. You can also go to work. No one will mind that, either. And Mullins won't mind as long as you leave the troops alone. Now get out of here and get packed. You're leaving tomorrow morning."

"But cousin Alex——"

"Move! I'm tired of the sight of you!" Alexander said.

Douglas turned and shambled out of the room. His ego was thoroughly deflated and he seemed more frightened than before. Obviously the Otpens weren't the pleasantest place in this world.

"They're a military post," Alexander said. "And Commander Mullins doesn't like Douglas. Can't say that I blame him. Douglas is a thoroughly unpleasant specimen, and incidentally quite typical of the rest of the Family." Alexander sighed and spread his hands in a gesture that combined disgust and resignation. "Sometimes I wonder why I have been cursed with my relatives."

Kennon nodded. The implications behind the empty eyes of Douglas's Lani sickened him. There were several ways to produce that expression, all of them unpleasant. Hypnoconditioning, the Quiet Treatment, brainburning, transorbital leukotomy, lobectomy—all of the products of that diseased period of humanity's thinking when men tampered with the brains of other men in an effort to cure psychic states. Psychiatry had passed that period, at least on the civilized worlds, where even animal experiments were frowned upon as unnecessary cruelty.

"You saw those two Lani," Alexander said. "Grandfather

had them made that way as a birthday present for Douglas. He was getting senile. He died a year later. You'd think a man would be ashamed to keep things like that around —but not Douglas. He *likes* them." Alexander's voice was tinged with contempt. "He knows they disgust me—so he parades them in. I could strangle that pup sometimes!"

"I wondered about it. I wouldn't like to work for a man who permitted such things."

"That was done before I took over. For the past three years there have been no dockings, no mutilations. I can't see treating a helpless animal like that."

"I feel better about it," Kennon said. "I didn't think you were that sort."

"Understand me," Alexander said. "I'm always opposed to senseless cruelty and waste—particularly when it's dangerous. Docked Lani are the height of stupidity. Just because someone wants a pet that is an exact duplicate of a human being is no reason to risk a court action. Those Lani, and a few others whose tails have been docked, could be a legal bombshell if they ever left Flora."

Kennon was jolted. He had been thinking of mental mutilation and Alexander had been talking physical. Naturally they would be dangerous property. Anyone attempting to sell a docked Lani would probably be thrown in Detention and charged with slave trading.

"Did you ever figure the cost of taking a legal action through our court system?" Alexander asked. "Even the small ones set you back four or five thousand, and a first-class action like a Humanity Trial could cost over a million. Grandfather found that out. Sure, there are differences between Lani and humans, but a smart lawyer can make them seem trivial until the final test and that would drag on for nearly two years until all the requirements were satisfied—and by that time the unfavorable publicity would drop sales to zero. The Family would be on my neck for lost dividends, and I'd lose much of the control I hold over them.

"Sure, it's possible that prehensile tails could be produced by mutation, but so far as we know it hasn't happened in human history. As a result, the tail serves as a trade-mark —something that can be easily recognized by anyone. So we sell them intact." Alexander crossed his legs and settled back in his chair. "Shocks you, doesn't it?"

Kennon nodded. "Yes," he admitted. "It does."

"I know. You can't help it. Most of our new employees think the Lani are human—at first. They learn better, but adjustment is always a strain. They keep confusing external appearances with the true article. But remember this—Lani are not human. They're animals. And on this island they're treated as what they are—no more, no less. They are a part of our economics and are bred, fed, and managed according to sound livestock principles. Despite some of the things you may see here in Alexandria, don't forget that. You are a veterinarian. Your job is to handle disease problems in animals. Lani are animals. Therefore you will be doing your job. I was disappointed in your reaction when you first saw them, but I suppose it was natural. At any rate this should clear the air."

"It does—intellectually," Kennon admitted. "But the physical resemblance is so close that it is difficult to accept."

Alexander smiled. "Don't worry. You'll accept it in time. Now I think it's time that you met the Family."

CHAPTER V

The main salon was crowded. The huge room, glittering with mirrors and crystal, floored with thick carpets, and hung with rich drapes, had something of the appearance of a Sarkian harem. Although there were only five of the Alexander family present, there were at least twenty Lani whose costumes ranged from the black G string and halter of the household staff to the utter nudity of Douglas's playthings. They were all female, and Kennon wondered for a moment what a male was like.

Besides Alexander, there were two men and three women: Douglas, still with his sulky expression, an older man in his late nineties who looked like Douglas's elder brother, two mature women who could be any age from fifty to three hundred, and a girl. She might have been thirty—perhaps younger, perhaps older, a lean feminine edition of Alexander, with the same intriguing face and veiled predatory look. There was a hardness about her that was absent in the others. Kennon had the feeling that whatever this girl did, she didn't do it half way.

"My sister Eloise," Alexander said in a low voice. "Watch

out for her. She's as deadly as a puff adder and she collects men. The other man is Douglas's father, Henry. The plump redhead beside him is his wife, Anne. The other woman is my mother, Clara, even though Eloise and I don't look like her. We take after Father."

"Where's he?" Kennon whispered.

"Dead," Alexander replied. "He was killed twenty years ago."

"I'd like to present Dr. Jac Kennon, our new veterinarian," Alexander said into the hush that followed their entrance. The introductions that followed were in proper form, and Kennon was beginning to feel more at ease until Eloise sent one of her Lani with a summons. He looked around for Alexander, but the entrepreneur was the center of a three-cornered argument, hemmed in by Douglas, Henry, and Anne. Henry's voice was raised in bitter protest that Alexander was exceeding his authority. He shrugged. There was no help there.

"All right," he said, "tell your mistress I'll be along in a moment."

"Yes, Doctor," the Lani said, "but the Woman Eloise says for you to come, and she is not accustomed to being disobeyed."

"Tell her what I said," Kennon replied. "I shall be there directly." He crossed to the table and examined it, selecting a cluster of odd purple fruit which looked more interesting than it tasted. When he had finished he walked leisurely over to where Eloise sat.

She looked at him angrily. "I am accustomed to being obeyed by my employees," she said coldly. Her dark eyes, oddly like her brother's, traversed his hard body like twin scanners.

He returned her appraising stare with one of his own. "I'm not your employee," he said bluntly. "I was hired by your brother, and there's a full peeper rider on my contract." His eyes traveled slowly over her carefully arranged hair, her make-up, her jewelry at throat and arms, her painted finger- and toenails, and then across the slim small-breasted lines of her body half revealed under her thin ankle-length tunic of Lyranian silk.

"Satisfied?" she asked.

"On Beta," he said bluntly, "your appearance would qualify you for a parasite camp. Six months of hard labor would do you no end of good. You're soft, lazy, and undisciplined."

Eloise gasped. "Why, you——" she sputtered.

25

"And perhaps next time you'll learn to be polite," Kennon continued imperturbably. "After all, the superficial attributes of good breeding are not too hard to counterfeit."

To his surprise, Eloise giggled. "You bite, don't you?" she asked. "Remind me to remember that."

"I shall."

"Of course, your actions weren't good breeding either."

"Admitted—but I've never pretended to be what I'm not. I'm the son of a spaceship skipper, and I'm a veterinarian. That's all."

"That's not all. You are also a man." Her face was sober. "It's been some time since I've met one. I'd almost forgotten they existed."

"There's your brother."

"Alex?—he's a money making machine. Come—sit beside me and let's talk."

"About what?"

"You—me—your job, your life—anything you wish."

"That line isn't exactly new," Kennon grinned.

"I know," she admitted, "but it usually works."

"I'm immune."

"That's what you think." Eloise's eyes were frankly appraising. "I think I could become interested in you."

"I have a job here. I don't think I would have time to give you the attention you'd demand."

"I get bored easily. It probably wouldn't be long before I would be tired of you."

"Perhaps—and perhaps not. I can't afford to take the chance."

"You seem confident."

"You forget. I was a sailor."

"And spacemen have a reputation, eh?" Eloise chuckled. "At that, you might be right. I remember the first officer of——" she let the thought die. "But I became tired of him," she finished.

Kennon smiled. "I've never had that complaint."

"Perhaps you'd like to make the acid test?" she asked.

"Perhaps," he said. "But not tonight."

"Tomorrow then? Alex will be leaving in the morning. He never stays more than a few hours." Eloise's eyes were bright, her lips moist and red.

"I'll pick the time," Kennon said—and added to himself, "If ever." Despite her wealth Eloise was no different than the port-of-call girls. If anything, she was worse since she had enough money to implement her desires. They were merely in the trade for business reasons. No—Eloise would be something to steer clear of. Alexander was right. She was a mantrap. He stood up and bowed Betan fashion. "I see your brother is free now. He wants to brief me on my duties here. We were discussing it before we entered."

Eloise pouted. "You can always do that."

"You said yourself that Alexander never stays here very long. I would be a poor employee if I delayed him." He grinned knowingly at her and she smiled back with complete understanding.

"Very well, then. Get your business done. Your pleasure can wait."

Kennon steered Alexander over to an open window that led to a balcony. "Whew!" he said. "I see what you mean."

"She's a tartar," Alexander agreed. "I suspect that she's a nymphomaniac."

"You suspect?" Kennon asked. "By this time you should know. Let's get out of here. I've had about all of your sister I care to take."

"Can't say as I blame you. I'll show you to your quarters. Maybe Old Doc left a bottle or two, although I suspect the old sinner hung on until the last one was empty."

"If he had to put up with your relatives as a steady diet, I can't say that I blame him," Kennon said.

"Careful, Doctor. You're talking about my kinfolk," Alexander said wryly. "At that, though, you have a point." The two men slipped quietly from the room. Apparently none of the Family was conscious of their departure except Eloise, who watched them leave with an enigmatic expression on her narrow face.

They left the fortress through the rear gate and walked slowly down the winding path that led to the cluster of buildings in the valley below. It was a beautiful night, calm and clear with the stars shining down from the dark vault of the heavens. The constellations were strange, and Kennon missed the moons. Beta had three, two of which were always in the sky, but Kardon was moonless. Somehow it gave the sky an empty look.

A damp coolness rose from the ground as the evening rain evaporated mistily into the still air. Kennon sniffed the odor of soil and growing vegetation, clean pleasant odors in contrast to what he had left. In the distance a bird called sleepily from one of the fortress turrets and was answered by some creature Kennon couldn't identify. A murmur of blended sound came from the valley below, punctuated by high-pitched laughter. Someone was singing, or perhaps chanting would be a better description. The melody was strange and the words unrecognizable. The thin whine of an atomotor in the fortress's generating plant slowly built up to a keening undertone that blended into the pattern of half-perceived sound.

"Nice, isn't it?" Alexander remarked as they rounded another turn on the switchback path.

"Yes. You can't hear a sound from back there except for that generator. It's almost as though we shut those people out of existence by merely closing a door."

"I wish it were that simple," Alexander said. "But doors that can be closed can also be opened. Well—think you'll like it here?"

"I think so, providing I don't have to entertain your relatives."

"You mean Eloise? Don't worry about her. She's as fickle as the wind."

"I've never seen anyone so frankly predatory," Kennon said. "She worries me."

"They'll all be gone tomorrow—except for Eloise," Alexander said with mock comfort. "Douglas is on the Otpens for a year, and the others are off somewhere."

"You'll be staying, I suppose."

"No—I'm afraid I can't."

"I hoped you'd help me get organized. This whole thing has been something of a shock. I was expecting something entirely different."

"Sorry—someone has to run the business. But Blalok'll brief you. Actually he's more qualified than I. He knows everything worth knowing about this place. We're going past his house in a minute—want to stop in and see him?"

"It's pretty late."

"Not for Blalok. He's a Mystic—a nocturnal. He's probably doing his work now."

"Perhaps we shouldn't disturb him."

"Nonsense. He's used to it. I visit him frequently at night."

"Sure—but you're the boss."

"Well—in a sense you are too. At least in the veterinary end of this business." Alexander swung sharply to the left and climbed a short flight of stairs that led to the nearest house. Lights flared on the deep porch, and the old-fashioned iris door dilated to frame the black silhouette of a stocky, broad-shouldered man.

"Good evening, sir," he said. "I was expecting you. That the new vet with you?"

"Your pipeline's still working, I see," Alexander said.

"Yes, this is Dr. Kennon—Evald Blalok—I wanted you two to meet."

Kennon liked the gray middle-aged man. He looked honest and competent, a solid quiet man with a craggy face and the deep-set eyes of a Mystic. His skin had the typical thickness and pore prominence of the dwellers on that foggy world from which he came. But unlike the natives of Myst, his skin was burned a dark brown by Kardon's sun. He seemed out of place on this tropic world, but Kennon reflected wryly that there was probably more than one misplaced human here, himself included.

"I've been going over Station Fourteen's records with Jordan," Blalok said as he ushered them into the house. A tall black-haired man rose as they entered.

"Skip the formality, Jordan. Sit down," Alexander said, "and meet Dr. Kennon—Steve Jordan—Jordan runs the Lani Division."

Kennon nodded acknowledgment as Alexander continued, "What's this trouble at Fourteen?"

"I don't know. We've got an epizootic of something. Another youngster died this morning, and there's three more that look pretty bad, jaundice, no appetite, complaining of muscular pains. Same symptoms as took the others. The one this morning makes the fourth this month, and we're only half through it."

"Are all your losses in this one station?" Kennon asked.

"No—but it's worst there."

"I don't like losses like that," Alexander said.

"Neither do I," Jordan replied.

"This isn't Jordan's fault, sir," Blalok said quickly. "As you know, we haven't had a vet for three months."

"Two," Alexander corrected.

"Three—Old Doc wasn't around at all the month before he died," Blalok said. "As a result we've got a problem. We need professional help."

"Well—here he is—use him," Alexander said. He looked at Kennon, a trace of amusement on his face. "There's nothing like getting into things early."

"Particularly when one comes into them stone cold," Kennon added. "It's a poor way to start a career."

"We can't afford to wait," Jordan said. "We need help."

"I'll see what can be done," Kennon replied. "Have you saved the body?"

"Every one of them," Jordan said. "They're in the hospital in the autopsy room."

29

"That was sensible. A post-mortem might give us an answer. Where's the hospital?"

"I'll show you," Jordan offered.

"Count me out," Alexander said. "I have a weak stomach."

"I'll go along if it's necessary," Blalok said.

"There's a staff there, Old Doc trained them," Jordan said.

"Then it shouldn't be necessary," Kennon said.

Blalok sighed with relief and turned to Alexander. "We could check the records while those two are about their bloody work."

"I'd rather check a long strong drink," Alexander replied. "What with the Family and this, it's too much to take for one evening."

Kennon hid a smile. Alexander had a weak spot. He was squeamish. That was a good thing to know.

CHAPTER VI

Jordan opened the door of the two-story building below Blalok's house. "This is it," he said, "just outside your front door. Convenient—no?"

"Too convenient," Kennon said, "also too quiet. Isn't anyone on duty?"

"I wouldn't know. Old Doc never kept the place open at night."

There was a stir of movement in the darkness, the lights flashed on, and a sleepy-eyed Lani blinked at them in the sudden glare. She looked blankly at Kennon and then brightened as she saw Jordan. "What's the trouble, sir?" she asked.

"Nothing. We want to look at the Lani I sent down this morning—Dr. Kennon would like to inspect the carcass."

"You're the new doctor?" the Lani asked. "Thank goodness you've come! I'll get the staff. I'll be back in a moment." She stepped quickly over to the switchboard beside the door and punched five buttons. Four more humanoids came into the room, followed a little later by a fifth.

"Where's the emergency?" one asked.

"He is—it's our new doctor."

"More females," Kennon muttered to himself. He turned to Jordan. "Aren't there any males in this crew?"

Jordan stared at him with mild surprise. "No, sir—didn't you know? There are no male Lani."

"*What?*"

"Just that," Jordan said. "Only females. There hasn't been a male on the island since Old Man Alexander took over. He killed them all."

"But that's impossible! How do they reproduce?"

"Ever hear of artificial fertilization?"

"Sure—but that's a dead end. The offspring are haploids and they're sterile. The line would die out in a generation."

"Not the Lani—you can see for yourself. We've been using the technique here for better than four centuries, and we're still doing all right. Over forty generations so far, and from the looks of things we can go on indefinitely."

"But how is it done?"

"I don't know. That's Alexander's secret. The Boss-man doesn't tell us everything. All I know is that we get results. Old Doc knew how it was done, and I suppose you will too, but don't ask me. I'm dumb."

Kennon shrugged. Maybe—maybe not. At any rate there was no sense in belaboring the point. He turned to the staff. Five of them were the same big-boned heavy-framed type that apparently did most of the manual labor. The sixth, the late arrival, was an elegant creature, a bronze-skinned, green-eyed minx with an elfin face half hidden under a wavy mass of red-brown hair. Unlike the others, she had been docked—and in contrast to their heavy eyes and sleep-puffed features she was alert and lively. She flashed him an impish grin, revealing clean white teeth.

Kennon smiled back. He couldn't help it. And suddenly the tension and strangeness was broken. He felt oddly at ease. "Which of you are on duty?" he asked.

"All of us," the redhead replied, "if it's necessary. What do you want us to do?"

"He's already told me. He wants that last carcass prepped for a post-mortem," the nightcall Lani said.

"Good," the redhead said. "It'll be nice to get to work again." She turned to face Kennon. "Now, Doctor—would you like to see your office? Old Doc left a fine collection of notes on Lani anatomy and perhaps you could do with a little review."

"I could do with a lot of it," Kennon admitted. "Unless the inner structure of a Lani is as similar to human as their outer."

"There are differences," the redhead admitted. "After all, we aren't quite alike."

"Perhaps I'd better do some reading," Kennon said.

"You need me any more?" Jordan asked.

"No—I think not."

"Good. I'll get back. Frankly, I don't like this any better than Blalok or the boss, but I'm low man on that pole. See you later."

Kennon chuckled as Jordan left. "Now, let's get ready for that cadaver," he said.

"Carcass, doctor," the redhead corrected. "A cadaver is a dead *human* body." She accented the "human."

Even in death there is no equality, Kennon thought. He nodded and the Lani led the way to a door which opened into a good-sized office, liberally covered with bookshelves. An old-fashioned plastic desk, some office cybernetics, a battered voicewriter, and a few chairs completed the furnishings. The redhead placed several large folio volumes in front of him and stepped back from the desk as he leafed rapidly through the color plates. It was an excellent atlas. Dr. Williamson had been a careful and competent workman.

Half an hour later, well fortified with a positional knowledge of Lani viscera, Kennon looked up at the redhead. She was still standing patiently, a statue of red-gold and bronze.

"Get a smock and let's go," he said. "No—wait a minute."

"Yes, sir?"

"What's your name? I don't want to say 'Hey you!'"

She smiled. "It's Copper Glow—want my pedigree too?"

"No—it wouldn't mean anything to me. Do they call you Copper or Glow? or both?"

"Just Copper, sir."

"Very well, Copper—let's get going."

The body of the dead Lani lay on the steel table, waxy and yellowish in the pitiless light of the fluorescents. She had been hardly more than a child. Kennon felt a twinge of pity—so young—so young to die. And as he looked he was conscious of another feeling.

It had been an open secret among his classmates that he had refused an offer to study human medicine because of his aversion to dissecting cadavers. The sarcoplastic models were all right, but when it came to flesh, Kennon didn't have the stomach for it. And now, the sight of the dead humanoid brought back the same cold sweat and gut-wrenching nausea that had caused him to turn to veterinary medicine eight years ago.

He fought the spasms back as he approached the table and made the external examination. Icterus and a swollen abdomen—the rest was essentially normal. And he knew with cold certainty that he could not lay a scalpel edge upon that cold flesh. It was too human, too like his own.

"Are you ready, Doctor?" the Lani standing across the table from him asked. "Shall I expose the viscera?"

Kennon's stomach froze. Of course! He should have realized! No pathologist did his own dissection. He examined. And that he could do. It was the tactile, not the visual sensations that upset him. He nodded. "The abdominal viscera first," he said.

The Lani laid back the skin and musculature with bold sure strokes. An excellent prosectress, Kennon thought. Kennon pointed at the swollen liver and the Lani deftly severed its attachments and laid the organ out for inspection. The cause of death was obvious. The youngster had succumbed to a massive liver-fluke infestation. It was the worst he had ever seen. The bile ducts were thick, calcified and choked with literally thousands of the gray-green leaf-shaped trematodes.

"Let's look at the others," he said.

Two more post-mortems confirmed the diagnosis. Except for minor differences, the lesions were identical. He removed a few of the flukes and set them aside for further study. "Well—that's that," he said. "You can clean up now."

He had found the criminal, and now the problem assumed the fascinating qualities of a crime hunt. Now he must act to prevent further murders, to reconstruct the crime, to find the *modus operandi*, to track the fluke to its source, and to execute it before it could do more harm.

Photographs and tri-dis would have to be taken, the parasite would have to be identified and its sensitivity to therapy determined. Studies would have to be made on its life cycle, and the means by which it gained entrance to its host. It wouldn't be simple, because this trematode was probably *Hepatodirus hominis*, and it was tricky. It adapted, like the species it parasitized.

Kennon leaned back from the microscope and studied the illustrations in the parasitology text. No matter how much *Hepatodirus* changed its life cycle, it could not change its adult form. The arrangements of the suckers and genital structures were typical. Old Doc's library on parasites was too inadequate for more than diagnosis. He would have to wait for his own books to be uncrated before he could do more than apply symptomatic treatment. He sighed and rose slowly to his feet. Tomorrow was going to be a busy day.

The door opened behind him and Copper slipped quietly into the office. She looked at him curiously, a faint half-shy smile on her face.

"What is it?" Kennon asked.

"Are you ready to fill out the autopsy protocol? It's customary."

"It's also customary to knock on a door before entering."

"Is it? Old Doc never mentioned it."

"I'm not Old Doc."

"No, you're not," she admitted. "You're much younger—and far more beautiful. Old Doc was a fat, gray old man." She paused and eyed Kennon appraisingly with a look on her pointed face that was the virtual twin of Eloise's. "I think I'll like working for you if you're as nice as you are pretty."

"You don't call a *man* beautiful or pretty!" Kennon exploded.

"Why not?"

"It just isn't done."

"You're a funny human," she said. "I called Old Doc beautiful, and he didn't mind."

"That's different. He was an old man."

"What difference does that make?"

"*I* don't like it," Kennon said, hitting on the perfect answer.

She stiffened. "I'm sorry, Doctor. I won't do it again." She looked down at him, head cocked sideways. "I guess I have a lot to learn about you. You're much different from Old Doc. *He* didn't snap at me." She paused for a moment, then drew a deep breath.

Kennon blinked.

"About that report," she said. "Regulations require that each post-mortem be reported promptly and that a record of the Lani concerned be posted in the death book together with all pertinent autopsy data. Man Blalok is very fussy about proper records." She drew one of the chairs to a spot beside the desk and sat down, crossed her long legs, and waited expectantly.

Kennon's mouth was suddenly dry. This situation was impossible. How in the name of Sir Arthur Fleming could he dictate a coldly precise report with a naked redhead sitting beside him? "Look," he said. "I won't need you. I can operate a voicewriter. You can pick up the material later and transcribe it."

Her face fell. "You don't like me," she said, her green eyes filling with quick tears. "Old Doc never——"

"Oh, *damn* Old Doc!" Kennon snapped. "And stop that sniveling—or get out. Better yet—get out *and* stop sniveling!"

She leaped to her feet and fled.

Kennon swore. There was no reason for him to act that way. He had been more brutal than necessary. But the girl—no, the Lani—was disconcerting. He felt ashamed of himself. He had behaved like a primitive rather than a member of one of the oldest human civilizations in the galaxy. He wouldn't bark at a dog that way. He shook his head. Probably he was tired. Certainly he was irritable, and unclad females virtually indistinguishable from human weren't the most soothing objects to contemplate.

He wondered if his exasperation was real or merely a defense mechanism. First Eloise, and then this! Confound it! He was surrounded! He felt trapped. And it wasn't because he'd been away from women too long. A week was hardly that. He grinned as he recalled the blonde from Thule aboard the starship. Now *there* was a woman, even though her ears were pointed and her arms were too long. She didn't pressure a man. She let him make the advances.

He grinned. That was it. He was on the defensive. He was the one who was being pursued—and his male ego had revolted. He shrugged and turned his attention to the autopsy report, but it was hopeless. He couldn't concentrate. He jotted a few notes and dropped them on the desk—tomorrow would be time enough. What he needed now was a stiff drink and eight hours' sleep.

CHAPTER VII

Kennon stopped at Blalok's house long enough to tell the superintendent what was causing the trouble. Blalok scowled. "We've never had flukes here before," he said. "Why should they appear now?"

"They've been introduced," Kennon said. "The thing that bothers me is how Dr. Williamson missed them."

"The old man was senile," Blalok said. "He was nearly blind the last six months of his life. I wouldn't doubt that he let his assistants do most of his work, and they could have missed them."

"Possibly, but the lesions are easy to see. At any rate, the culprit is known now."

"Culprit?"

"*Hepatodirus hominis*—the human liver fluke. He's a tricky little fellow—travels almost as far as men do."

"I'm glad it's your problem, not mine. All I can remember about flukes is that they're hard to eradicate."

"Particularly *H. hominis*."

"You can tell me about it later. Right now Mr. Alexander's over at Old—your house. Probably he's looking for you."

"Where's Jordan?"

"He went up to Station Fourteen. We'll see him tomorrow."

"I'll say good night then," Kennon said.

"I'm glad you're here. It's a load off my shoulders. See you tomorrow." Blalok waved a friendly good night and left the lights on long enough for Kennon to make his way to his quarters.

Alexander was seated in a heavily upholstered chair listening to a taped symphony in the stereo, his eyes half closed, an expression of peace on his face. An elderly Lani stood beside him. It was a comfortable picture.

The humanoid saw Kennon and gasped, a tiny indrawn sound of surprise. Alexander's eyes snapped open. "Oh—it's you," he said. "Don't worry, Kara—it's your new doctor."

Kara smiled. "You startled me," she said. "I was dreaming."

"On your feet?" Alexander interjected idly.

"I should have known you at once, Doctor. There's talk about you all over the yards, ever since you arrived."

"They know what is going on around here better than any of us," Alexander chuckled. "The grapevine is amazingly efficient. Well—what's the story?"

"Liver fluke."

"Hmm—not good."

"I think it can be stopped. I looked at the records. It doesn't seem to have been here too long."

"I hope you're right. How long will it take?"

"Several months, maybe a year, maybe more. I can't say. But I'll try to clean it up as quickly as possible. I'm pretty sure of the fluke, and it's a hard one to control."

"*Hepatodirus?*"

Kennon nodded.

"That's an offworld parasite, isn't it?"

"Yes. It originated on Santos. Parasitized the Varl originally, but liked humans better. It's adapted to a hundred different planetary environments, and it keeps spreading. It's a real cutie—almost intelligent the way it behaves. But it can be licked."

"Good—get on it right away."

"I'm starting tomorrow."

"Fine—I thought you'd be the right man. Kara! Fix the doctor a drink. We might as well have a nightcap—then I'll go back to the house and listen to Henry and Anne's screams about poor mistreated Douglas, and then back to Albertsville tomorrow. Duty and the credits call."

With mild surprise, Kennon realized that Alexander was drunk. Not obnoxiously, but enough to change his character. Intoxicated, he was a friendlier person. If there was any truth in the ancient cliché about alcohol bringing out a man's true character, then Alexander was basically a very nice person indeed.

"Well—here's your home for the next five years," Alexander said. "Eight rooms, two baths, a freshener, and three Lani to keep the place running. You've got it made."

"Perhaps—we'll see when we tackle this fluke infestation. Personally, I don't think I'm going to have an easy time. Tomorrow I'm going to be up to my neck in trouble trying to save your profits."

"You'll do it. I have confidence in you."

"I still think you should have hired a medic."

"This isn't all of your job," Alexander said. "And besides I can't afford to do it. Oh—not the money, but it might be admitting that the Lani might be human. And we've gone to a great deal of trouble to prove they're not." He shifted uncomfortably in his chair. "There's a story behind this."

"I wouldn't doubt it."

"Maybe it'd be better if I told it. It goes back over four centuries. Grandfather was a clever man. After he had secured this island he became worried about the surviving Lani. He didn't want to be accused of genocide, since the Lani were so human in appearance. So he had his medical officer make a few autopsies. The M.D. reported that while there was similarity, the Lani were probably not human.

"That was enough for Grandfather. He requested a Court of Inquiry. The court was sitting in Halsey and the hearing was private. Even so, it leaked and Grandfather was highly unpopular for a time until the lab reports came in. It cost him over eight hundred Ems and nearly two years' time to finish the case, but when it was over the Lani were declared alien, and Grandfather had ironclad discovery rights.

"They really put him through the mill. Grandfather furnished the bodies and three court-appointed M.O.'s went through them with microscopes. They didn't miss a thing. Their reports are so detailed that they're classics of their kind. They're almost required reading for anyone who wants to learn Lani structure and function. The court rendered an interim decision that the Lani were nonhuman, and armed with this, Grandfather prepared the final tests which were run by a team of court-appointed medics and biologists, who made *in vitro* and live tests on a number of Lani female prisoners. The tests ran for over two years and were totally negative. So the Alexander family acquired Flora and the Otpens, and a legal status." Alexander stood up. "Well—that's a capsule summary. The records are in the library if you'd care to check them."

"Why?"

"Just to prove we're honest." He moved carefully toward the door, opened it, and disappeared into the night.

Silently Kennon watched him descend the porch steps. He seemed steady enough. For a moment Kennon debated whether he should see him home—and then decided against it. If Alexander needed help he'd have asked for it. As it was, it was better to leave things alone. Certainly he didn't know Alexander well enough to act as a guardian. He turned back to the living area. The stereo was playing something soft and nostalgic as Kennon sank into the chair Alexander had vacated. He let his body relax. It had been as full a day as he had ever spent—filled with changes so abrupt that they were exhausting. He felt confused. There were no precedents he could apply. Neither his studies nor his travels had prepared him for living in a situation like this.

Legally and biologically the Lani weren't human. But they were intelligent, upright, bipedal mammals whose morphology was so close to man's that it had taken the ultimate test to settle their status. And being a Betan, Kennon was suspicious of the accuracy of that ultimate test.

But the Brotherhood of Man was based upon it. The feeling of unity that pervaded mankind's expanding empire was its product. From almost the beginning of mankind's leap to the stars it had been recognized that men must help each other or perish. The spirit of co-operation against the common enmity of alien worlds and cultures transcended the old petty rivalries on Earth. Men—all men—were brothers in arms.

And so the Brotherhood was born—and the concept born of necessity developed its muscles in a thousand battles on a thousand hostile worlds. And ultimately it evolved into the only form of central authority that men would accept. Yet basically it was not a government. It was an attitude of mind. Men accepted its decisions as they would accept the rulings of a family council, and for the same reasons.

The Brotherhood laid down certain rules but it did not attempt to enforce them. After all, it didn't need to. It also arbitrated disputes, admitted new worlds to membership, and organized concerted human effort against dangerous enemies. And that was all. Yet in its sphere the authority of the Brotherhood was absolute.

There was only one criterion for membership in the Brotherhood—membership in the human race. No matter how decadent or primitive a population might be, if it was human it was automatically eligible for Brotherhood—a free and equal partner in the society of human worlds.

Kennon doubted that any nonhuman race had ever entered the select circle of humanity, although individuals might have done so. A docked Lani, for instance, would probably pass unquestioned as a human, but the Lani race would not. In consequence they and their world were fair prey, and had been attacked and subjugated.

Of course, proof of inhumanity was seldom a problem. Most alien life forms were obviously alien. But there were a few—like the Lani—where similarities were so close that it was impossible to determine their status on the basis of morphology alone. And so the Humanity Test had come into being.

Essentially it was based upon species compatibility—on the concept that like can interbreed with like. Tests conducted on every inhabited world in the Brotherhood had proven this conclusively. Whatever changes had taken place in the somatic characteristics of mankind since the Exodus, they had not altered the compatibility of human germ plasm. Man could interbreed with man—aliens could not. The test was simple. The results were observable. And what was more important, everyone could understand it. No definition of humanity could be more simple or direct.

But was it accurate?

Like other Betans, Kennon wondered. It was—so far—probably. The qualifying phrases were those of the scientist, that strange breed that refuses to accept anything as an established fact until it is proven beyond a shadow of a doubt. After all, the human race had been spaceborne for only six thousand years—scarcely time for any real differences to develop. But physical changes had already appeared—and it would only be a question of time before these would probably be followed by genetic changes. And in some groups the changes might be extensive enough to make them genetic strangers to the rest of humanity.

What would happen then? No one knew. Actually no one bothered to think about it except for a few far-seeing men who worried as they saw.

Probably.

Might.

Possibly.

If.

Four words. But because of them the Betans were slowly withdrawing from the rest of humanity. Already the radiations of Beta's variant-G sun had produced changes in the population. Little things like tougher epidermis and depilation of body hair—little things that held alarming implications to Beta's scientists, and to Beta's people. Not too many generations hence a Betan outside his home system would be a rarity, and in a few millennia the Betan system itself would be a closed enclave peopled by humans who had deviated too far from the basic stock to mingle with it in safety.

Of course, the Brotherhood itself might be changed by that time, but there was no assurance that this would happen. And mankind had a history of dealing harshly with its mutants. So Beta would play it safe.

Kennon wondered if there were other worlds in the Brotherhood that had come to the same conclusion. Possibly there were. And possibly there were worlds where marked deviations had occurred. There wasn't a year that passed that didn't bring some new human world into the Brotherhood, and many of these had developed from that cultural explosion during the First Millennium known as the Exodus, where small groups of colonists in inadequate ships set out for unannounced goals to homestead new worlds for man. Some of these survived, and many were being discovered even at this late date. But so far none had any difficulty in proving their human origin.

The Lani, conceivably, could have been descendants of one of these groups, which probably explained the extreme care the Brotherhood courts had taken with their case. But they had failed the test, and were declared animals. Yet it was possible that they had mutated beyond genetic compatibility. If they had, and if it were proved, here was a test case that could rock the galaxy—that could shake the Brotherhood to its very foundations—that could force a re-evaluation of the criteria of humanity.

Kennon grinned. He was a fine employee. Here he was, less than a full day on the job, dreaming how he could ruin his employer, shake the foundation of human civilization, and force ten thousand billion humans to change their comfortable habit patterns and their belief in the unchangeable sameness of men. He was, he reflected wryly, an incurable romantic.

CHAPTER VIII

"Wake up, Doctor, it's six A.M." A pleasant voice cut through Kennon's slumber. He opened one eye and looked at the room. For a moment the strange surroundings bothered him, then memory took over. He stirred uncomfortably, looking for the owner of the voice.

"You have your morning calls at seven, and there's a full day ahead," the voice went on. "I'm sorry, sir, but you should get up." The voice didn't sound particularly sorry.

It was behind him, Kennon decided. He rolled over with a groan of protest and looked at his tormentor. A gasp of dismay left his lips, for standing beside the bed, a half smile on her pointed face, was Copper—looking fresh and alert and as disturbing as ever.

It wasn't right, Kennon thought bitterly, to be awakened from a sound sleep by a naked humanoid who looked too human for comfort. "What are you doing here?" he demanded.

"I'm supposed to be here," Copper said. "I'm your secretary." She grinned and flexed a few curves of her torso.

Kennon was silent.

"Is there anything wrong?" she asked.

For a moment Kennon was tempted to tell her what was wrong—but he held his tongue. She probably wouldn't understand. But there was one thing he'd better settle right now. "Now look here, young lady—" he began.

"I'm not a lady," Copper interrupted before he could continue. "Ladies are human. I'm a Lani."

"All right," Kennon growled. "Lani or human, who cares?

But do you have to break into a man's bedroom and wake him in the middle of the night?"

"I didn't break in," she said, "and it isn't the middle of the night. It's morning."

"All right—so it's morning and you didn't break in. Then how in Halstead's sacred name did you get here?"

"I sleep next door," she said jerking a thumb in the direction of an open door in the side wall. "I've been there ever since you dismissed me last night," she explained.

The explanation left Kennon cold. The old cliché about doing as the Santosians do flicked through his mind. Well, perhaps he would in time—but not yet. The habits of a lifetime couldn't be overturned overnight. "Now you have awakened me," he said, "perhaps you'll get out of here."

"Why?"

"I want to get dressed."

"I'll help you."

"You will *not!* I'm perfectly capable of taking care of myself. I've been dressing myself for years. I'm not used to people helping me."

"My—what a strange world you must come from. Haven't you ever had a Lani before?"

"No."

"You poor man." Her voice was curiously pitying. "No one to make you feel like the gods. No one to serve you. No one to even scrub your back."

"That's enough," Kennon said. "I can scrub my own back."

"How?—you can't reach it."

Kennon groaned.

"Weren't there *any* Lani on your world?"

"No."

"No wonder you left it. It must be quite primitive."

"Primitive!" Kennon's voice was outraged. "Beta has one of the highest civilizations in the Brotherhood!"

"But you don't have Lani," she said patiently. "So you must be primitive."

"Halstead, Fleming, and Ochsner!" Kennon swore. "Do you *believe* that?"

"Naturally, isn't it obvious? You can't possibly be civilized unless you take responsibility for intelligent life other than your own race. Until you face up to your responsibilities you are merely a member of a dominant race, not a civilized one."

Kennon's reply caught in his throat. His eyes widened as he looked at her, and what he was about to say remained unspoken. "Out of the mouths of humanoids—" he muttered oddly.

"What does that mean?" Copper asked.

"Forget it," Kennon said wildly. "Leave me alone. Go put on some clothes. You embarrass me."

"I'll go," Copper said, "but you'll have to be embarrassed. Only household Lani wear cloth." She frowned, two vertical furrows dividing her dark brows. "I've never understood why inhouse Lani have to be disfigured that way, but I suppose there's some reason for it. Men seldom do anything without a reason."

Kennon shook his head. Either she was grossly ignorant, which he doubted, or she was conditioned to the eyeballs. The latter was more probable. But even that was doubtful. Her trenchant remark about civilization wasn't the product of a conditioned mind. But why was he worrying about her attitudes? They weren't important—she wasn't even human. He shook his head. That was a sophistry. The fact that she wasn't human had nothing to do with the importance of her attitude. "I suppose there is a reason," he agreed. "But I don't know it. I haven't been here long enough to know anything about such things."

She nodded. "That does make a difference," she admitted. "Many new men are bothered at first by the fact that we Lani are naked, but they adjust quickly. So will you." She smiled as she turned away. "You see," she added over her shoulder as she left the room, "we're not human. We're just another of your domestic animals."

Was there laughter in her voice? Kennon wasn't sure. His sigh was composed of equal parts of relief and exasperation as he slipped out of bed and began to dress. He'd forgo the shower this morning. He had no desire for Copper to appear and offer to scrub his back. In his present state of mind he couldn't take it. Possibly he'd get used to it in time. Perhaps he might even like it. But right now he wasn't acclimatized.

"Man Blalok called," Copper said as she removed the breakfast dishes. "He said that he'd be right over to pick you up. He wants to show you the operation."

"When did he call?"

"About ten minutes ago. I told him that you were at breakfast. He said he'd wait." She disappeared in the direction of the kitchen.

"There's a nightmare quality to this," Kennon muttered as he slipped his arms into the sleeves of his tunic and closed the seam tabs. "I have the feeling that I'm going to wake up any minute." He looked at his reflection in the dresser mirror, and his reflection looked worriedly back. "This whole thing has an air of plausible unreality: the advertisement, the contract, this impossible island that raises humanoids as part of the livestock." He shrugged and his mirrored image shrugged back. "But it's real, all right. No dream could possibly be this detailed. I wonder how I'm going to take it for the next five years? Probably not too well," he mused silently. "Already I'm talking to myself. Without even trying, that Lani Copper can make me feel like a Sarkian." He nodded at his image.

The Sarkian analogy was almost perfect, he decided. For on that grimly backward world females were as close to slaves as the Brotherhood would permit; raised from birth under an iron regimen designed to produce complaisant mates for the dominant males. Probably that was the reason Sark was so backward. The men, having achieved domestic tranquillity, had no desire to do anything that would disturb the status quo. And since no Sarkian woman under any conceivable circumstances would annoy her lordly master with demands to produce better mousetraps, household gadgetry, and more money, the technological development of Sark had come to a virtual standstill. It took two sexes to develop a civilization.

Kennon shrugged. Worlds developed as they did because people were as they were, and while passing judgment was still a major human pursuit, no native of one world had a right to force his customs down the unwilling throat of another. It would be better to accept his present situation and live with it rather than trying to impose his Betan conception of morality upon Lani that neither understood nor appreciated it. His business was to treat and prevent animal disease. What happened to the animals before infection or after recovery was none of his affair. That was a matter between Alexander and his conscience.

Blalok was waiting for him, sitting behind the wheel of a square boxy vehicle that squatted with an air of unpolished efficiency on the graveled drive behind his house. He smiled a quick greeting as Kennon approached. "It's about time you showed up," he said. "You'll have to get into the habit of rising early on this place. We do most of our work early in the morning and late in the afternoon. During the day it's too hot to breathe, let alone work. Well, let's get going. There's still time to visit the outer stations."

Kennon climbed in and Blalok started the vehicle. "I

thought we'd take a jeep today," he said. "They aren't very pretty, but they get around." He turned onto the surfaced road that ran down the hill toward the hospital and the complex of red-roofed buildings clustered about it. "About those flukes," he said. "You have any plans to get rid of them?"

"Not yet. I'll have to look the place over. There's more detective work than medicine involved in this."

"Detective work?"

"Sure—we know the criminal, but to squelch him we have to learn his hangouts, study his *modus operandi*, and learn how to make his victims secure from his activities. Unless we do that, we can treat individuals from now to infinity and all we'll have is more cases. We have to apply modern criminology tactics—eliminate the source of crime —stop up the soft spots. In other words, kill the flukes before they enter the Lani."

"Old Doc never said anything about this," Blalok said.

"Probably he never knew about it. I was looking over the herd books last night, and I saw nothing about trematodes, or anything that looked like a parasite pattern until the last few months."

"Why not?"

"My guess is that he was one of the first deaths."

"You mean this thing attacks human beings?"

"Preferentially," Kennon said. "It's strange, too, because it originated on Santos so far as we know. In fact, some people think that the Varl bred it for a weapon to use against us before we conquered them. They could have done it. Their biological science was of a high enough order."

"But how did it get here?"

"I wouldn't know—unless you've hired a Santosian or someone else who was affected."

"We did have a man from Santos. Fellow called Joe Kryla. We had to let him go because he was a nudist. It made a bad impression on the Lani. But that was over a year ago."

"That's about the right time to build up a good reservoir of infection. The fatal cases usually don't show up before an area is pretty well seeded."

"That's not so good."

"Well, there's one thing in our favor. The Lani are pretty well concentrated into groups. And so far there doesn't seem to be any infestation outside of Hillside Station— except for two deaths in Lani recently sent from there.

If we quarantine those stations and work fast, maybe we can stop this before it spreads all over the island."

"That's fine, but what are you going to do now?"

"Treat those that show symptoms. There should be some Trematox capsules at the hospital. If there aren't we'll get them. We'll take the sick ones back to the hospital area and push therapy and supportive treatment. Now that we know the cause, we shouldn't have any more death losses."

"Old Doc didn't treat at the hospital," Blalok said.

"I'm not Old Doc."

"But it's going to mess up our operations. We're using the ward buildings to finish training the Lani scheduled for market."

"Why?"

"It's convenient. Most of the ward space is filled right now." Blalok said. There was a touch of disgust in his voice.

"They're well, aren't they?" Kennon demanded.

"Of course."

"Then get them out of there."

"But I told you——"

"You told me nothing. The hospital area is needed for something more than a training center. Perhaps Old Doc was trained in outcall work, but I'm not. I work from a hospital. The only things I do on outcalls are diagnoses, vaccinations, and emergencies. The rest of the patients come to the hospital."

"This isn't going to set well with Jordan and the division chiefs."

"That's not my concern," Kennon said. "I run my business in the best way possible. The patients are of more concern than the personal comfort of any straw boss or administrator. You're the administrator—you calm them down."

"You have the authority," Blalok admitted. "But my advice to you is to go slow."

"I can't," Kennon said. "Not if we want to prevent any more losses. There simply won't be time to run all over the island dosing with Trematox and taking temperatures, and while that sort of thing is routine, it should be supervised. Besides, you'll see the advantages of this method soon enough."

"I hope so," Blalok said as he braked the jeep to a stop in front of the hospital. "I suppose you'll want to take some things along."

"So I will," Kennon said. "I'll be back in a minute." Kennon slid from the seat, leaving Blalok looking peculiarly at his departing back.

The minute stretched to nearly ten before Kennon returned followed by two Lani carrying bags which they loaded into the back of the jeep. "I had to reorganize a little," Kennon apologized, "some things were unfamiliar."

"Plan on taking them?" Blalok said, jerking a thumb at the two Lani.

"Not this time. I'm having them fit up an ambulance. They should be busy most of the day."

Blalok grunted and started the turbine. He moved a lever and the jeep floated off the ground.

"An airboat too," Kennon remarked. "I wondered why this rig was so boxy."

"It's a multipurpose vehicle," Blalok said. "We need them around here for fast transport. Most of the roads aren't so good." He engaged the drive and the jeep began to move. "We'll go cross country," he said. "Hillside's pretty far out—the farthest station since we abandoned Olympus."

The air began whistling past the boxlike body of the jeep as Blalok increased the power to the drive and set the machine on automatic. "We'll get a pretty good cross-section of our operations on this trip," he said over the whine of the turbine. "Look down there."

They were passing across a series of fenced pastures and Kennon was impressed. The size of this operation was beginning to sink in. It hadn't looked so big from the substratosphere in Alexander's ship, but down here close to the ground it was enormous. Fields of grain, wide orchards, extensive gardens. Once they were forced to detour a huge supply boat that rose heavily in front of them. Working in the fields were dozens of brown-skinned Lani who paused to look up and wave as the jeep sped by. Occasional clusters of farm buildings and the low barrackslike stations appeared and disappeared behind them.

"There's about twenty Lani at each of these stations," Blalok said, "They work the farm area under the direction of the stationmaster."

"He's a farmer?"

"Of course. Usually he's a graduate of an agricultural school, but we have a few who are descendants of the crew of the first Alexander, and there's one old codger who was actually with him during the conquest. Most of our stationmasters are family men. We feel that a wife and children add to a man's stability—and incidentally keep him from fooling around with the Lani."

A series of fenced pastures containing hundreds of huge grayish-white quadrupeds slipped past.

"Cattle?" Kennon asked.

"Yes—Earth strain. That's why they're so big. We also have sheep and swine, but you won't see them on this run."

"Any native animals?"

"A few—and some which are native to other worlds. But they're luxury-trade items. The big sale items are beef, pork, and mutton." Blalok chuckled. "Did you think that the Lani were our principal export?"

Kennon nodded.

"They're only a drop in the bucket. Agriculture—Earth-style agriculture—is our main source of income. The Lani are valuable principally to keep down the cost of overhead. Virtually all of them work right here on the island. We don't sell more than a hundred a year—less than five per cent of our total. And those are surplus—too light or too delicate for farm work."

"Where do you find a market for all this produce?" Kennon asked.

"There's two hundred million people here, and quite a few billion more in space-train range. We can produce more cheaply than any competitor, and we can undersell any competition, even full automation." Blalok chuckled. "There are some things that a computer can't do as well as a human being, and one of them is farm the foods on which humanity is accustomed to feed. A man'll pay two credits for a steak. He could get a *Chlorella* substitute for half a credit, but he'll still buy the steak if he can afford it. Same thing goes for fruit, vegetables, grain, and garden truck. Man's eating habits have only changed from necessity. Those who can pay will still pay well for natural foods." Blalok chuckled. "We've put quite a dent in the algae and synthetics operations in this sector."

"It's still a luxury trade," Kennon said.

"You've eaten synthetic," Blalok replied. "What do *you* prefer?"

Kennon had to agree that Blalok was right. He, too, liked the real thing far better than its imitations.

"If it's this profitable, then why sell Lani?" Kennon asked.

"It's the Family's idea. Actually—since the export type is surplus it does us no harm. We keep enough for servants —and the others would be inefficient for most farm work. So disposal by sale is a logical and profitable way of culling. But now the Boss-man is being pressured into breeding an export type. And this I don't like. It's too commercial. Smells like slavery."

"You're a Mystic, aren't you?" Kennon asked.

"Sure—but that doesn't mean I like slavery. Oh, I know some of those fatheaded Brotherhood economists call our system economic slavery—and I'll admit that it's pretty hard to crack out of a spherical trust. But that doesn't mean that we *have* to stay where we are. Mystics aren't owned by their entrepreneurs. Sure, it's a tough haul to beat the boss, but it can be done. I did it, and others do it all the time. The situation isn't hopeless."

"But it is with the Lani," Kennon added.

"Of course. That's why they should be protected. What chance does a Lani have? Without us they can't even keep going as a race. They're technological morons. They don't live long enough to understand modern civilization. To turn those poor helpless humanoids out into human society would be criminal. It's our duty to protect them even while we're using them."

"Man's burden?" Kennon said, repeating the old cliché.

"Exactly." Blalok scowled. "I wish I had guts enough to give the Boss-man the facts—but I can't get nerve enough to try. I've a good job here—a wife and two kids—and I don't want to jeopardize my future." Blalok glanced over the side. "Well, here we are," he said, and began descending into the center of a spokelike mass of buildings radiating outward from a central hub.

"Hmm—big place," Kennon murmured.

"It should be," Blalok replied. "It furnishes all of our Lani for replacement and export. It can turn out over a thousand a year at full capacity. Of course we don't run at that rate, or Flora would be overpopulated. But this is a big layout, like you said. It can maintain a population of at least forty thousand. Old Alexander had big ideas."

"I wonder what he planned to do with them?" Kennon said.

"I wouldn't know. The Old Man never took anyone into his confidence."

Jordan came up as the jeep settled to the ground. "Been expecting you for the past half hour," he said. "Your office said you were on your way.—Good to see you, too, Doc. I've been going over the records with Hank Allworth—the stationmaster here." Jordan held out his hand.

"You're an Earthman, eh?" Kennon asked as he grasped the outstretched hand. The gesture was as old as man, its ritualistic meaning lost in antiquity.

"No—Marsborn—a neighbor world," Jordan said. "But our customs and Earth's are the same."

"You're a long way from home," Kennon said.

"No farther than you, Doc." Jordan looked uncomfortable. "But we can compare origins later. Right now, you'd better come into the office. I've run across something peculiar."

CHAPTER IX

"There are twelve bays to this station," Jordan said. "Under our present setup two are used for breeding and the other ten for maturation. We rotate the youngsters around the bay—a different bay each year until they're age eleven. Then they're sorted according to type and sent out for a year of further specialized training after which they go onto the farms, or to inhouse or export.

"Now here's the peculiar part. There's no trouble in Bays One through Nine, but Bay Ten has had all our losses except two that have occurred at the training stations."

"That's good news," Kennon said. "Our parasite can't have had time to migrate too far. We have him pinpointed unless —say how many training centers are there?"

"Three," Jordan said.

"Quarantine them," Kennon replied. "Right now. Nothing goes in or out until we've checked them and completed prophylaxis."

Jordan looked at Blalok inquiringly.

"He's the boss," Blalok said. "Do as you're told. This is his problem."

"Why the quarantine?" Jordan asked.

"I want to get any carriers. We can check them with antigen, and then give Trematox."

"All that concentration in Bay Ten," Jordan said. "Does it mean something?"

"Blalok said that there was a Santosian in your division."

"Yeah—Joe Kryla—and come to think of it, he ran Bay Ten!"

"That's a help—now let's see what makes that bay different from the others."

"Why?"

"I'll tell you—but you may not understand," Kennon said.

"I'll take a chance."

Kennon grinned. "All right, you asked for it. The parasite that's doing the damage is a flatworm, a trematode called *Hepatodirus hominis*. As I've told Blalok, it's a tricky thing. Like all trematodes it has a three-stage life cycle, but unlike every other fluke, its life cycle is not fixed to definite intermediate hosts. Depending upon where it is, the fluke adapts. It still must pass through its life cycle, but its intermediate host need not be one species of snail, fish, or copepod. Any cold-blooded host will do. What you have here is a Kardonian variant which has adapted to some particular intermediate host on this world. Until now, its final host was either man or Varl. Now we have a third, the Lani. And apparently they are the most susceptible of the three. It never kills Varl. And humans, while they're more susceptible, only occasionally succumb, but the Lani appear to be the most susceptible of all. I've never seen an infestation like those Lani had. Their livers were literally crawling with flukes." Kennon paused and looked at Jordan. "You following me?" he asked.

"Slowly and poorly," Jordan said. "You're assuming too much knowledge on my part."

Kennon chuckled. "You can't say I didn't warn you."

"Well—I'm really interested in only one thing—how do you break the parasite up in business?"

"There's only one sure way—and that's to break the life cycle. The technique is thousands of years old, but it's just as good today as it was then."

"Good—then let's do it."

"To make a varrit stew," Kennon said, "one must first catch the varrit."

"Huh?"

"We have to learn the beastie's life cycle before we can break it, and like I said, it adapts. Its intermediate host can be any one of a hundred cold-blooded animals."

"Is there no place else where it can be attacked?"

"Sure, in the body of the final host, or on its final encysting place. But that won't eliminate the bug."

"Why not?"

"It'll still survive in its infective form and enough Lani will get subacute dosage to propagate it until the time is right for another epizootic. We have to kill its intermediate host—or hosts if it has more than one. That will keep it from growing and will ultimately eradicate it."

Judson scratched his head. "It sounds complicated."

"It is. It's so complicated that once the fluke becomes well established it's virtually impossible to eradicate."

"And you think it can be done here?"

"We can give it the old college try. But it's going to take some detective work."

"Where do we start?"

"With Bay Ten. We look it over real well. Then we check the diet and habits of the Lani. Then we check each individual Lani. Then we check the life cycle of the parasite. Somewhere along the line if we're lucky we'll find a weak point that can be attacked."

"That's a big order," Blalok said.

"It can't be helped. That's the way it is. Of course, we're lucky that we're on an isolated land mass. That gives us an advantage. We should be able to clean this up."

"How long do you think it will take?"

"It depends on how well the fluke is established. Six months at the minimum—and I wouldn't care to guess at the maximum. However, I hope the minimum will be time enough."

"So do I," Blalok said.

"Well," Kennon said, "let's get on with it."

"I hope it won't interrupt our program," Jordan said.

"Of course it will interrupt it," Kennon replied. "It can't help it. Get the idea in your head that you're facing something here that can cripple you—maybe abort your whole operation. You have a choice—interrupt now or abort later. And half measures won't work. To eradicate this pest requires an all-out effort."

"But I can't see why we can't merely bypass Bay Ten—" Jordan said.

"Take my word for it," Kennon said. "You can't. There's no accurate way of telling how far this spreads until the death losses occur. Our tests for fluke infestation aren't that good. We have to work thoroughly and carefully. We can't be butting heads over this—either we all co-operate or this whole operation will blow up in our faces.

"Look at the record. Six months ago you ended a year with no deaths from disease. Five months ago Old Doc and two Lani were ill. Four months ago one of the two Lani was dead and Old Doc was too ill to be effective. Three months ago Old Doc and the other Lani were dead, and before the end of the month two more followed them. Two months ago six died, last month eight, and so far this month you've lost four and you have over two weeks to go. Up to now they've all been from here, but two this month were at other stations.

In six months if nothing is done, we'll be having losses there unless we're lucky. And the losses will keep on increasing. Apparently you don't know what it is to live with parasites—so let me tell you. It isn't pleasant!"

Blalok shrugged. "You needn't get hot about it," he said. "After all, you're the Doc—and we'll co-operate."

Jordan nodded. "We will," he said. "All the way."

CHAPTER X

There is a special providence that looks over recent veterinary graduates, Kennon reflected as he checked the monthly reports from the Stations. Since the time he had laid down the law to Judson and Blalok, he had had no trouble from the production staff. And for the past four months there had been no further trouble with *Hepatodirus*. That unwanted visitor had apparently been evicted. At that, they had been lucky. The parasite had been concentrated at Hillside Station and had failed to establish itself in the training area. The intermediate host, it had turned out, was a small amphibian that was susceptible to commercial insecticide. It had been no trouble to eradicate. Systemic treatment and cooking of all food had cleaned up the infective cercaria and individual infections, and after six months of intensive search, quarantine, and investigation, Kennon was morally certain that the disease had been eradicated. The last four reports confirmed his belief.

He sighed as he leaned back in his chair. Blalok was at last convinced that his ideas were right. The hospital was operating as a hospital should, with a staff of twelve Lani kept busy checking the full wards. Actually, it was working better than it should, since stationmasters all over the island were now shipping in sick animals rather than treating them or requesting outpatient service.

"Hi, Doc," Blalok said as he pushed the door open and looked into the office. "You doing anything?"

"Not at the moment," Kennon said. "Something troubling you?"

"No—just thought I'd drop in for a moment and congratulate you."

"For what?"

"For surviving the first year."

"That won't be for two months yet."

Blalok shook his head. "This is Kardon," he said. "There's only three hundred and two days in our year, ten thirty-day months and two special days at the year's end."

Kennon shrugged. "My contract is Galactic Standard. I still have two months to go. But how come the ten-month year? Most other planets have twelve, regardless of the number of days."

"Old Alexander liked thirty-day months."

"I've wondered about that."

"You'll find a lot more peculiar things about Flora when you get to know her better. This year has just been a breaking-in period."

Kennon chuckled. "It's damn near broken me," he admitted. "You know, I thought that the Lani'd be my principal practice when I came here."

"You didn't figure that right. They're the easiest part. They're intelligent and co-operative."

"Which is more than one can say about the others." Kennon wiped the sweat from his face. "What with this infernal heat and their eternal stubbornness, I've nearly been driven crazy."

"You shouldn't have laid out that vaccination program."

"I had to. Your hog business was living mostly on luck, and the sheep and shrakes were almost as bad. You can't get away from soil saprophytes no matter how clean you are. Under a pasture setup there's always a chance of contamination. And that old cliché about an ounce of prevention is truer of livestock raising than anything else I can think of."

"I have some more good news for you," Blalok said. "That's why I came over. We're going to have another species to treat and vaccinate."

Kennon groaned. "Now what?"

"Poultry." Blalok's voice was disgusted. "Personally I think it's a mess, but Alexander thinks it's profitable. Someone's told him that pound for pound chickens are the most efficient feed converters of all the domestic animals. So we're getting a pilot plant: eggs, incubator, and a knocked-down broiler battery so we can try the idea out. The Boss-man is always hot on new ideas to increase efficiency and production. The only trouble is that he fails to consider the work involved in setting up another operation."

"You're so right. I'll have to brush up on pullorum,

ornithosis, coccidiosis, leukosis, perosis, and Ochsner knows how many other -osises and -itises. I was never too strong on fowl practice in school, and I'd be happier if I never had anything to do with them."

"So would I," Blalok agreed. "I can't see anything in this but trouble."

Kennon nodded.

"And he's forgotten something else," Blalok added. "Poultry need concentrated feed. We're going to have to install a feed mill."

Kennon chuckled. "I hope he'll appreciate the bill he gets."

"He thinks we can use local labor," Blalok said gloomily. "I wish he'd realize that Lani are technological morons."

"They could learn."

"I suppose so—but it isn't easy. And besides, Allworth is the only man with feed-mill experience, and he's up to his ears with Hillside Station since that expansion order came in."

"I never did get the reason for that. After we complained about the slavery implications and got the Boss-man's okay to hold the line, why do we need more Lani?"

"Didn't you know? His sister's finally decided to try marriage. Found herself some overmuscled Halsite who looked good to her—but she couldn't crack his moral barrier." Blalok grinned. "I thought you'd be the first to know. Wasn't she interested in you?"

Kennon chuckled. "You could call it that. Interested—like the way a dog's interested in a beefsteak. It's a good thing we had that fluke problem or I'd have been chewed up and digested long ago. That woman frightens me."

"I could be scared by uglier things," Blalok said. "With the Boss-man's sister on my side I wouldn't worry."

"What makes you think she'd be on my side? She's a cannibal."

"Well, you know her better than I do."

He did—he certainly did. That first month had been one of the worst he had ever spent, Kennon reflected. Between Eloise and the flukes, he had nearly collapsed—and when it had come to the final showdown, he thought for a while that he'd be looking for another job. But Alexander had been more than passably understanding and had refused his sister's passionate pleas for a Betan scalp. He owed a debt of gratitude to the Boss-man.

"You're lucky you never knew her," Kennon said.

"That all depends on what you mean," Blalok said as he grinned and walked to the door. The parting shot missed its mark entirely as Kennon looked at him with blank incomprehension. "You should have been a Mystic," Blalok said. "A knowledge of the sacred books would do you no end of good." And with that cryptic remark the superintendent vanished.

"That had all the elements of a snide remark," Kennon murmured to himself, "but my education's been neglected somewhere along the line. I don't get it." He shrugged and buzzed for Copper. The veterinary report would have to be added to the pile already before him, and the Boss-man liked to have his reports on time.

Copper watched Kennon as he dictated the covering letter, her slim fingers dancing over the stenotype. He had been here a full year—but instead of becoming a familiar object, he had grown so gigantic that he filled her world. And it wasn't merely because he was young and beautiful. He was kind, too.

Yet she couldn't approach him, and she wanted to so desperately that it was a physical pain. Other Lani had told her about men and what they could do. Even her old preceptress at Hillside Station had given her some advice when Man Allworth had tattooed the tiny V on her thigh that meant she had been selected for the veterinary staff. And when Old Doc had brought her from the Training Station to the hospital and removed her tail, she was certain that she was one of the lucky ones who would know love.

But love wasn't a pain in the chest, an ache in the belly and thighs, an unfulfilled longing that destroyed sleep and made food tasteless. Love was supposed to be pleasant and exciting. She could remember every word her preceptress had spoken.

"My little one," the old Lani had said, "you now wear the doctor's mark. And soon no one will be able to tell you from a human. You will look like our masters. You will share in their work. And there may be times when you will find favor in their eyes. Then you may learn of love.

"Love," the old voice was soft in Copper's ears. "The word is almost a stranger to us now, known only to the few who serve our masters. It was not always so. The Old Ones knew love before Man Alexander came. And our young were the fruit of love rather than the product of our masters' cunning. But you may know the flower even though you cannot bear its fruit. You may enter that world of pleasure-pain the Old Ones knew, that world which is now denied us.

"But remember always that you are a Lani. A man may be kind to you. He may treat you gently. He may show you love. Yet you never will be his equal. Nor must you become too attached to him, for you are not human. You are not his natural mate. You cannot bear his young. You cannot completely share. You can only accept.

"So if love should come to you, take it and enjoy it, but do not try to possess it. For there lies heartache rather than happiness. And it is a world of heartache, my little one, to long for something which you cannot have."

To long for something which one cannot have! Copper knew that feeling. It had been with her ever since Kennon had come into her life that night a year ago. And it had grown until it had become gigantic. He was kind—yes. He was harsh—occasionally. Yet he had shown her no more affection than he would have shown a dog. Less—for he would have petted a dog and he did not touch her.

He laughed, but she was not a part of his laughter. He needed her, but the need was that of a builder for a tool. He liked her and sometimes shared his problems and triumphs with her, and sometimes his defeats, but he did not love. There had never been for her the bright fierce look he had bent upon the Woman Eloise those times when she had come to him, the look men gave to those who found favor in their eyes.

Had he looked at her but once with that expression she would have come to him though fire barred the way. The Woman Eloise was a fool.

Copper looked at him across the corner of the desk, the yellow hair, the bronze skin, firm chin, soft lips and long straight nose, the narrowed eyes, hooded beneath thick brows, scanning the papers in his lean-tendoned hands. His nearness was an ache in her body—yet he was far away.

She thought of how his hands would feel upon her. He had touched her once, and that touch had burned like hot iron. For hours she had felt it. He looked up. Her heart choked her with its beating. She would die for him if he would but once run his fingers over her tingling skin, and stroke her hair.

The naked emotion in Copper's face was readable enough, Kennon thought. One didn't need Sorovkin techniques to interpret what was in her mind. And it would have been amusing if it weren't so sad. For what she wanted, he couldn't give. Yet if she were human it would be easy. A hundred generations of Betan moral code said "never," yet when he looked at her their voices faded. He was a man—a member of the ruling race. She was an animal—a beast—a humanoid—near human but not near enough. To like her was easy—

but to love her was impossible. It would be bestiality. Yet his body, less discerning than his mind, responded to her nearness.

He sighed. It was a pleasant unpleasantness, a mixed emotion he could not analyze. In a way it was poetry—the fierce, vaguely disquieting poetry of the sensual Santosian bards—the lyrics that sung of the joys of flesh. He had never really liked them, yet they filled him with a vague longing, an odd uneasiness—just the sort that filled him now. There was a deadly parallel here. He sighed.

"Yes, sir? Do you want something?" Copper asked.

"I could use a cup of coffee," he said. "These reports are getting me down." The banality amused him—sitting here thinking of Copper and talking about coffee. Banality was at once the curse and the saving grace of mankind. It kept men from the emotional peaks and valleys that could destroy them. He chuckled shakily. The only alternative would be to get rid of her—and he couldn't (*or wouldn't?*—the question intruded slyly) do that.

Copper returned with a steaming cup which she set before him. Truly, this coffee was a man's drink. She had tried it once but the hot bitterness scalded her mouth and flooded her body with its heat. And she had felt so lightheaded. Not like herself at all. It wasn't a drink for Lani. Of that she was certain.

Yet he enjoyed it. He looked at her and smiled. He was pleased with her. Perhaps—yet—she might find favor in his eyes. The hope was always there within her—a hope that was at once fear and prayer. And if she did—she would know what to do.

Kennon looked up. Copper's face was convulsed with a bright mixture of hope and pain. Never, he swore, had he seen anything more beautiful or sad. Involuntarily he placed his hand upon her arm. She flinched, her muscles tensing under his finger tips. It was though his fingers carried a galvanic current that backlashed up his arm even as it stiffened hers.

"What's the matter, Copper?" he asked softly.

"Nothing, Doctor. I'm just upset."

"Why?"

There it was again, the calm friendly curiosity that was worse than a bath in ice water. Her heart sank. She shivered. She would never find her desire here. He was cold—cold—cold! He wouldn't see. He didn't care. All right—so that was how it had to be. But first she would tell him. Then he could do with her as he wished. "I hoped—for the past year that you would see me. That you would think of me not as a Lani, but as a beloved." The words came faster now, tumbling over one another. "That you would desire me and take me to those worlds we cannot know unless you humans show us. I have hoped so much, but I suppose it's wrong— for you—you are so very human, and I—well, I'm not!" The last three words held all the sadness and the longing of mankind aspiring to be God.

"My dear—my poor child," Kennon murmured.

She looked at him, but her eyes could not focus on his face, for his hands were on her shoulders and the nearness of him drove the breath from her body. From a distance she heard a hard tight voice that was her own. "Oh, sir—oh *please*, sir!"

The hands withdrew, leaving emptiness—but her heartbeat slowed and the pink haze cleared and she could see his face.

And with a surge of terror and triumph she realized what she saw! That hard bright look that encompassed and possessed her! The curved lips drawn over white, white teeth! The flared nostrils! The hungry demand upon his face that answered the demand in her heart! And she knew—at last— with a knowledge that turned her limbs to water, that she had found favor in his eyes!

CHAPTER XI

Mixed emotion! Ha! The author of that cliché didn't even know its meaning! Kennon strode furiously down the dusty road toward Station One trying to sublimate his inner conflict into action. It was useless, of course, for once he stopped moving the grim tug-of-war between training and desire would begin again, and no matter how it ended the result would be unsatisfactory. As long as he had been able to delude himself that he was fond of Copper the way a man is fond of some lesser species, it had been all right. But he knew now that he was fond of her as a man is of a woman—and it was hell! For no rationalization in the universe would allow him to define her as human. Copper was humanoid—something *like* human. And to live with her and love her would not be miscegenation, which was bad enough, but bestiality which was a thousand times worse.

Although throughout most of the Brotherhood miscegenation was an unknown word, and even bestiality had become a loose definition on many worlds with humanoid populations, the words had definite meaning and moral force to a Betan. And—God help him—he was a Betan. A lifetime of training in a moral code that frowned upon mixed marriages and shrank appalled from even the thought of mixing species was nothing to bring face to face with the fact that he loved Copper.

It was odd, Kennon reflected bitterly, that humans could do with animals what their customs and codes prohibited them from doing to themselves. For thousands of years— back to the very dawn of history when men had bred horses and asses to produce mules—men had been mixing species to produce useful hybrids. Yet a Betan who could hybridize plants or animals with complete equanimity shrank with horror from the thought of applying the same technique to himself.

What was there about a human being that was so sacrosanct? He shook his head angrily. He didn't know. There was no answer. But the idea—the belief—was there, ingrained into his attitudes, a part of his outlook, built carefully block by block from infancy until it now towered into a mighty wall that barred him from doing what he wished to do.

It would be an easier hurdle if he had been born anywhere except on Beta. In the rest of the Brotherhood, the color of a man's skin, the shape of his face, the quality and color of his hair and eyes made no difference. All men were brothers. But on Beta, where a variant-G sun had already caused genetic divergence, the brotherhood of man was a term that was merely given lip service. Betans were different and from birth they were taught to accept the difference and to live with it. Mixing of Betan stock with other human species, while not actually forbidden, was so encircled with conditioning that it was a rare Betan indeed who would risk self-opprobrium and the contempt of his fellows to mate with an outsider. And as for humanoids—Kennon shuddered. He couldn't break the attitudes of a lifetime. Yet he loved Copper.

And she knew he did!

And that was an even greater horror. He had fled from the office, from the glad light in her eyes, as a burned child flees fire. He needed time to think, time to plan. Yet his body and his surface thoughts wanted no plans or time. Living with a Lani wasn't frowned upon on Flora. Many of the staff did, nor did anyone seem to think less of them for doing so. Even Alexander himself had half-confessed to a more than platonic affection for a Lani called Susy.

Yet this was no excuse, nor would it silence the cold still voice in his mind that kept repeating *sodomite—sodomite—sodomite* with a passionless inflection that was even more terrible than anger.

The five kilometers to Station One disappeared unnoticed beneath his feet as he walked, and he looked up in surprise to see the white walls and red roofs of the station looming before him.

"Good Lord! Doc! What's got into you?" the stationmaster said. "You look like you'd seen a ghost. And out in this sun without a helmet! Come inside, man, before you get sunstroke!"

Kennon chuckled without humor. "Getting sunstroke is the least of my worries, Al," he said, but he allowed Al Crothers to usher him inside.

"It's odd that you showed up right now," Al said, his dark face showing the curiosity that filled him. "I just had a call from Message Center not five minutes ago, telling me to have you call in if you showed up."

Kennon sighed. "On this island you can't get away from the phone," he said wryly. "O.K., where is it?"

"You look pretty bushed, Doc. Maybe you'd better rest awhile."

"And maybe it's an emergency," Kennon interrupted. "And probably it is because the staff can handle routine matters—so maybe you'd better show me where you keep the phone."

"One moment please," the Message Center operator said. There were a few clicks in the background. "Here's your party," she continued. "Go ahead, Doctor."

"Kennon?" a nervous voice crackled from the receiver.

"Yes?"

"You're needed out on Otpen One."

"Who is calling—and what's the rush?"

"Douglas—Douglas Alexander. The Lani are dying! It's an emergency! Cousin Alex'll skin us alive if we let these Lani die!"

Douglas! Kennon hadn't thought of him since the one time they had met in Alexandria. That was a year ago. It seemed much longer. Since the Boss-man had exiled his cousin to that bleak rock to the east of Flora there had been no word of him. And now—he laughed a sharp bark of humorless annoyance—Douglas couldn't have timed it better if he had tried!

"All right," Kennon said. "I'll come. What seems to be the trouble?"

"They're sick."

"That's obvious," Kennon snapped. "Otherwise you wouldn't be calling. Can't you tell me any more than that?"

"They're vomiting. They have diarrhea. Several have had fits."

"Thanks," Kennon said. "I'll be right out. Expect me in an hour."

"So you're leaving?" Al asked as he cradled the phone.

"That's a practitioner's life," Kennon said. "Full of interruptions. Can I borrow your jeep?"

"I'll drive you. Where do you want to go?"

"To the hospital," Kennon said. "I'll have to pick up my gear. It's an emergency all right."

"You're a tough one," Al said admiringly. "I'd hate to walk five kilos in this heat without a hat—and then go out on a call."

Kennon shrugged. "It's not necessarily toughness. I believe in doing one job at a time—and my contract reads veterinary service, not personal problems. The job comes first and there's work to do."

Copper wasn't in sight when Kennon came back to the hospital—a fact for which he was grateful. He packed quickly, threw his bags into the jeep, and took off with almost guilty haste. He'd contact the Hospital from the Otpens. Right now all he wanted was to put distance between himself and Copper. Absence might make the heart grow fonder, but at the moment propinquity was by far the more dangerous thing. He pointed the blunt nose of the jeep toward Mount Olympus, set the autopilot, opened the throttle, and relaxed as best he could as the little vehicle sped at top speed for the outer islands. A vague curiosity filled him. He'd never been on the Otpens. He wondered what they were like.

Otpen One was a rocky tree-clad islet crowned with the stellate mass of a Class II Fortalice. But this one wasn't like Alexandria. It was fully manned and in service condition.

"Airboat!" a voice crackled from the dashboard speaker

of the jeep, "Identify yourself! You are being tracked."

Kennon quickly flipped the IFF switch. "Dr. Kennon, from Flora," he said.

"Thank you, sir. You are expected and are clear to land. Bring your vehicle down in the marked area." A section of the roof turned a garish yellow as Kennon circled the building. He brought the jeep in lightly, setting it carefully in the center of the area.

"Leave your vehicle," the speaker chattered. "If you are armed leave your weapon behind."

"It's not my habit to carry a gun," Kennon snapped.

"Sorry, sir—regulations," the speaker said. "This is S.O.P."

Kennon left the jeep and instantly felt the probing tingle of a search beam. He looked around curiously at the flat roof of the fortress with its domed turrets and ugly snouts of the main battery projectors pointing skyward. Beside him, the long metal doors of a missile launcher made a rectangular trace on the smooth surface of the roof. Behind him the central tower poked its gaunt ferromorph and durilium outline into the darkening sky bearing its crown of spiderweb radar antennae turning steadily on their gimbals covering a vast hemisphere from horizon to zenith with endless inspection.

From the base of the tower a man emerged. He was tall, taller even than Kennon, and the muscles of his body showed through the tightness of his battle dress. His face was harsh, and in his hands he carried a Burkholtz magnum—the most powerful portable weapon mankind had yet devised.

"You are Dr. Kennon?" the trooper asked.

"I am."

"Your I.D., please."

Kennon handed it over and the big man scanned the card with practiced eyes. "Check," he said. "Follow me, sir."

"My bags," Kennon said.

"They'll be taken care of."

Kennon shrugged and followed the man into the tower. A modern grav-shaft lowered them to the ground floor. They passed through a gloomy caricature of the Great Hall in Alexandria, through an iris, and down a long corridor lined with doors.

A bell rang.

"Back!" the trooper said. "Against the wall! Quick! Into the doorway!"

"What's up?"

"Another practice alert." The trooper's voice was bored. "It gets so that you'd almost wish for a fight to relieve the monotony."

A trooper and several Lani came down the corridor, running in disciplined formation. Steel clanged on steel as they turned the corner and moments later the whine of servos came faintly to their ears. From somewhere deep in the pile a rising crescendo of generators under full battle load sent out vibrations that could be sensed rather than heard. A klaxon squawked briefly. There was another clash of metal, and a harsh voice boomed through the corridors. "Fourteen seconds. Well done. Secure stations!"

The trooper grinned. "That ties the record," he said. "We can go now."

The corridor ended abruptly at an iris flanked by two sentries. They conferred briefly with Kennon's guide, dilated the iris, and motioned for Kennon to enter. The pastel interior of the modern office was a shocking contrast to the gray ferromorph corridors outside.

Douglas Alexander was standing behind the desk. He was much the same. His pudgy face was haggard with uncertainty and his eyes darted back and forth as his fingers caressed the knobby grip of a small Burkholtz jutting from a holster at his waist. There were new, unpleasant furrows between his eyes. He looked older and the indefinable air of cruelty was more pronounced. He had been frightened the last time Kennon had seen him, and he was frightened now.

"I'm not sure whether I am glad to see you, Kennon," he said uncertainly. "But I suppose I have to be."

Kennon believed him.

"How have you been?" Kennon asked.

"Not too bad until this afternoon. Things have been going pretty well." He shifted uncomfortably from one foot to another. "I suppose Cousin Alex will skin me for this, but there's nothing else I can do." He licked his lips. "You've been here long enough—and you'll have to know eventually." He fidgeted and finally sat down behind the desk. "We have trouble. Half the Lani were stricken about four hours ago. It was sudden. No warning at all. And if they die——" his voice trailed off.

"Well—what are we waiting for? Get someone to bring my bags down here and we'll look them over."

"Do you have to?—Can't you prescribe something?"

"How? I haven't examined the patients."

"I can tell you what's wrong."

Kennon smiled. "I hardly think that's the way to do it. Even though your description might be accurate, you still might miss something of critical importance."

Douglas sighed. "I thought that's what you'd say," he said. "Oh—very well—you might as well see what we have out here."

"You can't possibly believe that I don't already know," Kennon said. "You have male Lani."

Douglas looked at him, his face blank with surprise. "But —how did you know? No one on the main island does except the Family. And we never talk about it. Did Eloise tell you? I noticed she was struck with you the day you came, and the Lani who have come out here since have been talking about you two. Did she do it?"

Kennon shook his head. "She never said a word."

"Then how——"

"I'm not stupid," Kennon said. "That story you've spread about artificial fertilization has more holes in it than a sieve. That technique has been investigated a thousand times. And it has never worked past the first generation. If you had been using it, the Lani would long ago have been extinct. Haploids don't reproduce, and the only way the diploid number of chromosomes can be kept is to replace those lost by maturation division of the ovum. You might be able to keep the diploid number by using immature ova, but the fertilization technique would be far more complex than the simple uterine injections you use at Hillside Station."

Douglas looked at him blankly.

"Besides," Kennon added, "I have a microscope. I checked your so-called fertilizing solution. I found spermatozoa, and spermatozoa only come from males. What's more, the males have to be the same species as the females or fertilization will not take place. So there must be male Lani. Nothing else fits. You've been using artificial insemination on the main-island Lani. And from the way this place is guarded, it's obvious that here is your stud farm."

Douglas shrugged and spread his hands in a gesture of resignation. "I suppose," he said, "that's the way Old Doc found out too. We never told him, but he knew before he ever came out here."

"The only thing that puzzles me," Kennon went on, "is how you managed to eliminate the Y-chromosome carriers within the sperm."

"Eh?"

"The male sex-determinant. Half the sperm carry it, but

so far as I know, there's never been a male born on the main island."

"Oh—that. It's something that's done in the labs here. Probably one of the technicians could tell you. It's called electro—electro freezing or something like that."

"Electrodiaphoresis?"

Douglas nodded. "That sounds like it. I don't know anything about it. One of Grandfather's men did the basic work. We just follow instructions." He shrugged. "Well—since you know the secret there's no sense in hiding the bodies. Come along and tell me what's wrong."

It was a peculiar feeling to walk down the row of cubical rooms with their barred doors. The whole area reminded him of a historical novel, of the prisons of early human history where men confined other men for infractions of social customs. The grimness of the place was appalling. The male Lani—impressive in their physical development—were in miserable condition, nauseated, green-faced, retching. The sickening odors of vomit and diarrhea hung heavily on the air. Douglas coughed and held a square of cloth to his face, and even Kennon, strong-stomached as he was, could feel his viscera twitch in sympathy with the caged sufferers.

"Great Fleming, man!" Kennon exploded. "You can't keep them here. Get them out! Give them some fresh air! This place would make a well man sick."

Douglas looked at him, "I wouldn't take one of them out unless I had him shackled and there was an armed guard to help me. Those males are the most vicious, cunning, and dangerous animals on Kardon. They exist with but one thought in mind—to kill!"

Kennon looked curiously through a barred door at one of the Lani. He lay on a bare cot, a magnificently muscled figure with a ragged black beard hiding his face. There were dozens of scars on his body and one angry purple area on his thick right forearm where flesh had been torn away not too long ago. Beads of sweat stood out on his forehead and soft moaning noises came from his tight lips as he pressed his abdomen with thick-fingered hands. "He doesn't look so dangerous," Kennon said.

"Watch it!" Douglas warned. "Don't get too close!" But the warning was too late. Kennon touched the bars, and as he did, the Lani moved with fluid speed, one huge hand clutching Kennon's sleeve and pulling him against the bars while the other darted for his throat. Fingers bit into Kennon's neck and tightened in a viselike grip.

Kennon reacted automatically. His arms came up inside the Lani's and crashed down, elbows out, tearing the Lani loose. He jumped back, rubbing his bruised throat. "That fellow's not sick!" he gasped. "He's crazy!"

The Lani glared at him through the bars, disappointment written on his scarred and bearded face.

"I warned you," Douglas said. His voice held an undertone of malicious laughter. "He must be sick or he would have killed you. George is clever in a stupid sort of way."

Kennon looked into the cubicle. The Lani glared back and growled. There was a beastlike note in his voice that made the short hairs on Kennon's neck prickle.

"That fellow needs a lesson," he said.

"You want to give it to him?" Douglas asked.

"Not particularly."

"Ha!—man!—you afraid!" the Lani taunted. His voice was thick and harsh. "All men fear me. All Lani, too. I am boss. Come close again man and I kill you!"

"Are they all that stupid?" Kennon asked. "He sounds like a homicidal moron."

"He's not stupid," Douglas said. "Just uneducated."

"Why is he so murderous?"

"That's his training. All his life he has fought. From childhood his life has been based on his ability to survive in an environment where every male is his enemy. You see here the sublimation of individuality. He cannot co-operate with another male. He hates them, and they in turn hate him. George, here, is a perfect example of absolute freedom from restraint." Douglas smiled unpleasantly.

"His whole history is one of complete lack of control. As an infant, being a male, his mother thought she was favored by the gods and she denied him nothing. In fact we were quite insistent that she gave him everything he wanted. By the time he was able to walk and take care of himself, he was completely spoiled, selfish, and authoritative.

"Then we took him and a dozen others exactly like him and put them together." Douglas grinned. "You should see what happens when a dozen spoiled brats are forced to live together. It's more fun. The little beasts hate each other on sight. And we stimulate them to compete for toys, food, and drink. Never quite enough to go around. You can imagine what happens. Instead of sharing, each little selfish individualist fights to get everything he can grab. Except for one thing we don't punish them no matter what they do. If anyone shows signs of co-operating he is disciplined severely, the first time. The next time, he is culled.

But other than that, we leave them alone. They develop their personalities and their muscles—and if one proves to be too much for his fellows we transfer him to a more advanced class where the competition is keener, and he learns what it is to lose.

"At puberty we add sex drive to the basics, and by the time our male reaches maturity we have something like George. Actually, George is more mature than either you or I. He has all the answers he needs. He's strong, solitary, authoritative, and selfish. He has no curiosity and resents encroachment. He's a complete individualist. If he proves out he should make an excellent sire."

"But isn't he dangerous to handle?" Kennon asked.

"Yes, but we take precautions."

Kennon grimaced with distaste.

"Look at it objectively," Douglas said. "We're trying to select the best physical type we can in the hope that he'll pass his qualities to his offspring, and there's no better practical way to select the strongest and hardiest than by natural selection. We control their environment as little as possible and let Nature do our educating until they're old enough to be useful.

"Naturally, there are some things which we cannot provide, such as exposure to disease, to the elements, and to predators. The one isn't selective about whom it infects, while the others would tend to produce co-operation as a matter of survival."

"Isn't there a great deal of mortality under such a regimen?" Kennon asked.

"Not as much as you might expect. It's about twenty per cent. And there is a great deal of compensation from a management viewpoint. We get essentially the same physical end product as we would from a closely managed operation, plus a great saving in labor. Males, you see, are fairly expendable. We only need a few a year."

"It's brutal."

"So it is, but life is brutal. Still, it's efficient for our purposes. We merely take advantage of natural impulses to produce a better product. Grandfather got the idea out of an old book—something about the noble savage, natural selection and survival of the fittest. He thought it was great—said there was nothing like relentless competition to bring out the strongest and hardiest types. And he's been right for centuries. Can you imagine anything much better than George—from a physical viewpoint?"

"He is a magnificent animal," Kennon admitted as he eyed the Lani. "But it seems to me that you could train some obedience into him."

Douglas shook his head. "That would introduce a modifying factor, something bigger and more powerful than the male himself. And that would modify the results. We can control them well enough with knockout gas and shackles. And those things, oddly enough, don't destroy their pride or self-esteem. They think that we use them because we are afraid, and it satisfies their egos."

Kennon eyed the caged Lani dubiously. "This is going to be difficult. I must examine them and treat them, but if they're all as homicidal as this one——"

"You fight me man," George interrupted, his face twisted into lines of transparent guile. "I am boss and others do as I say. You beat me, then you are boss."

"Is this true?" Kennon asked.

"Oh, it's true enough," Douglas said. "George is the leader and if you beat him you'd be top male until some other one got courage enough to challenge you. But he's just trying to get his hands on you. He'd like to kill."

Kennon looked at the big humanoid appraisingly. George was huge, at least five centimeters taller and fifteen kilograms heavier than himself. And he was all muscle. "I don't think I'd care to accept that challenge unless I was forced to," Kennon said.

Douglas chuckled. "I don't blame you."

Kennon sighed. "It looks like we are going to need reinforcements to get these brutes under control. I'm not going in there with them, and I can't examine them from out here."

"Oh, we can hold them all right. Paralysis gas and shackles will keep them quiet. There's no need to bother the troopers. We can handle this by ourselves."

Kennon shrugged. "It's your baby. You should know what you're doing."

"I do," Douglas said confidently. "Wait here until I get the gas capsules and the equipment." He turned and walked back to the entrance to the cell block. At the iris he turned. "Be careful," he said.

"Don't worry, I will." Kennon looked at George through the bars and the humanoid glared back, his eyes bright with hatred. Kennon felt the short hairs prickle along the back of his neck. George roused a primal emotion—an elemental dislike that was deeper than reason—an antagonism intensely physical, almost overpowering—a purely adrenal response that had no business in the make-up of a civilized human.

He had thought the Lani had a number of human traits until he had encountered George. But if George was a typical male—then the Lani were alien. He flexed his muscles and stared coldly into the burning blue eyes behind the bars. There would be considerable satisfaction in beating this monstrosity to a quivering pulp. Millennia of human pre-eminence —of belief that nothing, no matter how big or muscular, should fail to recognize that a man's person was inviolate— fed the fuel of his anger. The most ferocious beasts on ten thousand worlds had learned this lesson. And yet this animal had laid hands on him with intent to kill. A cold corner of his mind kept telling him that he wasn't behaving rationally, but he disregarded it. George was a walking need for a lesson in manners.

"Don't get the idea that I'm afraid of you—you over-muscled oaf," Kennon snapped. "I can handle you or anyone like you. And if you put your hands on me again I'll beat you within an inch of your worthless life."

The Lani snarled. "Let me out and I kill you. But you are like all men. You use gun and iron—not fair fight."

Douglas returned with a gas capsule and a set of shackles. "All right," he said. "We're ready for him." He handed Kennon the shackles and a key to the cell door—and drew his Burkholtz.

"See," the Lani growled. "It is as I say. Men are cowards."

"You know gun?" Douglas asked as he pointed the muzzle of the Burkholtz at the Lani.

"I know," George growled. "Gun kill."

"It does indeed," Douglas said. "Now get back—clear back against the wall."

George snarled but didn't move.

"I'll count three," Douglas said, "and if you're not back by then I'll burn you down. You'll obey even if you won't do anything else—one—two——"

George retreated to the far end of his cell.

"Now face the wall." Douglas tossed the gas capsule into the cell. The thin-walled container broke, releasing a cloud of vapor. George crumpled to the floor. "Now we wait a couple of minutes for the gas to dissipate," Douglas said. "After that he's all yours. You can go in and put the irons on him."

"Will he be out long?" Kennon asked.

"About five minutes. After that he'll have muscular control." Douglas chuckled. "They're stupid," he said. "They know what gas does to them, but they never have sense enough to hold their breath. They could be twice as much trouble as they are. All right, it's safe to go in now." Douglas let the gun dangle in his hand.

Kennon unlocked the door.

And George rolled over, muscles bunched and driving! He hit the door with such force that Kennon was slammed against the wall, dazed—half stunned by the speed of the attack. George—he had time to think in one brief flash—wasn't stupid. He had held his breath for the necessary two minutes!

Douglas jerked the blaster up and fired, but his target was too quick. George dropped and rolled. The sizzling streak of violet flashed inches above his body and tore a six-inch hole through the back of the cell. And then George was on him! The huge, marvelously fast hands of the humanoid wrenched the blaster out of Douglas's hands and jerked him forward. A scream burst from Douglas as George's hands closed around his neck. Muscles sprang into writhing life in the humanoid's huge forearms. There was a soft, brittle crack, and Douglas sagged limp in the iron grip that held him dangling.

"Faugh!" George grunted. He dropped Douglas as Kennon pushed the door back and came out into the passageway. "Maybe you make better fight," George said as he lowered his head into the muscular mass of his broad shoulders.

Kennon eyed him appraisingly, swinging the irons in his right hand.

This time the Lani didn't charge. He moved slowly, half crouched, long arms held slightly forward. Kennon backed away, watching the humanoid's eyes for that telltale flicker of the pupils that gives warning of attack. The expression on George's face never changed. It was satisfied—smug almost—reflecting the feelings of a brute conditioned to kill and given an opportunity to do so. The Lani radiated confidence.

Kennon shivered involuntarily. He wasn't frightened, but he had never met an opponent like this. A chill raced up the back of his legs and spread over his stomach and chest. His mouth was dry and his muscles quivered with tense anticipation. But his concentration never wavered. His hard blue eyes never left George's, searching with microscopic intentness for the faintest sign of the Lani's intentions.

George charged—hands reaching for Kennon's throat, face twisted in a snarl of rage and hate. But even as he charged

Kennon moved. He ducked beneath the Lani's outstretched hands and drove his left fist deep into George's belly just below the breastbone.

Air whistled out of the Lani's gaping mouth as he bent double from the power of the blow. Kennon clipped him on the chin with a driving knee, snapping George's head back and smashed the bearded face with the shackles. Blood spurted and George screamed with rage. One of the Lani's big hands wrapped around the shackles and tugged. Kennon let go and drove another left to George's ribs.

The Lani threw the irons at Kennon, but his aim was poor. One of the handcuff rings scraped across Kennon's cheek, but did nothing more than break the skin. Half paralyzed by the blows to his solar plexus, George's co-ordination was badly impaired. But he kept trying. Kennon wrapped lean fingers about one of George's outstretched hands, bent, pivoted, and slammed the Lani with bone-crushing force against the bars of a nearby cell. But George didn't go down. "He's more brute than man," Kennon thought. "No man could take a beating like that!" He moved aside from George's stumbling rush, feeling a twinge of pity for the battered humanoid. It was no contest. Strong as he was, George didn't know the rudiments of hand-to-hand fighting. His reactions were those of an animal, to close, clutch, bite, and tear. Even if he were completely well, the results would have been the same. It would merely have taken longer. Kennon drove a vicious judo chop to the junction of the Lani's neck and shoulder. Brute strength was no match for the highly evolved mayhem that every spaceman learns as a necessary part of his trade. George had never been on planet leave in a spaceport town. He knew nothing about the dives, the crimps, the hostile port police. His idea of fighting was that of a beast, but Kennon was a civilized man to whom fighting was an art perfected by millennia of warfare. And Kennon knew his trade.

Even so it took longer than Kennon expected because George was big, George was strong, and George had courage and pride that kept him coming as long as the blazing will behind his blazing eyes could drive his battered body. But the end was inevitable.

Kennon looked at his bloody arm where George's teeth had reached their mark. It was hardly more than a scratch, but it had been close. George had his lesson and Kennon felt oddly degraded. He sighed, dragged George back into the cell, and locked the door.

Then he turned to Douglas. The howls of hate from the caged Lani died to a sullen silence as Kennon gently examined the limp body.

Douglas wasn't dead. His neck was dislocated, not broken, but he was in serious condition. Kennon was still bending over Douglas wondering how to call for help when three guards burst through the door, faces grim, weapons at the ready.

"What's going on here?" the leader demanded. "The board showed an open door down here." He saw the body—"Mr. Douglas!" he gasped. "The commandant will have to know about this!" He took a communicator from his waist belt and spoke rapidly into it. "Arleson in stud cell block," he said. "Attempted escape. One casualty—Douglas Alexander—yes, that's right. No—he's not dead. Send a litter and bearers. Inform the commandant. I am making investigation on the spot. Out." He turned to look coldly at Kennon.

"Who are you—and what happened here?" he asked.

Kennon told him.

"You mean you took *George!*" Arleson said.

"Look in his cell if you don't believe me."

The soldier looked and then turned back to Kennon. There was awed respect in his hard brown eyes.

"You did *that!*—to *him!* Man, you're a fighter," he said in an unbelieving voice.

A stretcher detail manned by two sober-faced Lani females came in, loaded Douglas's body on the stretcher, and silently bore it away.

"Douglas was a fool," Arleson said. "He knew we never handle this kind without maximum restraint. I wonder why he did it?"

"I couldn't say. He told me that gas and shackles would hold him."

"He knew better. These Lani know gas capsules. All George had to do was hold his breath. In that cell George would have killed you. You couldn't have stayed away from him."

Kennon shrugged. Maybe that was what Douglas had wanted. Kennon sighed. He didn't have the answer. And it could just be that Douglas had tried to show off. Well, he would pay for it. He'd have a stiff neck for months, and perhaps that was a proper way to end it.

Commander Mullins, a thin gray-faced man with the hard cold eyes of a professional soldier, came into the corridor followed by another trooper.

His eyes took in the wreckage that had been George, the split lips, the smashed nose, the puffed eyes, the cuts and bruises, and then raked across Kennon.

"Spaceman—hey?" he asked. "I've seen work like that before."

Kennon nodded. "I was once. I'm station veterinarian now. Douglas called me over—said it was an emergency."

Mullins nodded.

"Well—why aren't you tending to it?"

"I have to examine them," Kennon said gesturing at the cells. "And I don't want any more trouble like this."

"Don't worry. You won't have it. Now that you've beaten George, you'll have no trouble at all. You're top dog." Mullins gestured at the cages. "They'll be good for a while. Now you'd better get on with your work. There's been enough disruption of routine for today. The men will help you."

Kennon checked in at the commandant's office before he left for the main island.

"How is Douglas?" he asked.

"He's alive," Mullins said. "We flew him to Albertsville—and good riddance. How are the Lani?"

"They'll be all right," Kennon said. "It's just food poisoning. I suggest you check your kitchen and your food handlers. There's a break in sanitation that could incapacitate your whole command. I found a few things wrong but there are probably more."

"I'll check on it—and thanks for the advice," Mullins said. "Sit down, Doctor. Your airboat won't be serviced for another few minutes. Tell me how things are on the main island. How's Blalok?"

"You know him?"

"Of course. I used to be a frequent visitor there. But with that young pup here, I couldn't leave. I didn't dare to. He'd have disrupted routine in a single day. Look what he did in half an hour. Frankly, I owe you a debt for getting him off my hands." Mullins chuckled dryly.

"That's a fine thing to say," Kennon grinned. "But I can sympathize. It took us two months to straighten out Alexandria after the Boss-man sent him here."

"I heard about that."

"Well—we're under control now. Things are going pretty smoothly."

"They'll be better here," Mullins said. "Now that Douglas is gone." He shrugged. "I hope the Boss doesn't send him back. He's hard to handle and he makes discipline a problem."

"Could you tell me—or would it be violating security?" Kennon said. "Why do you have a Class II installation on full war footing out here?"

Mullins chuckled. "It's no secret," he said. "There was a commercial raid on this place about fifty years ago. Seems as though one of our competitors didn't like us. Alexandria was on a war footing then and managed to hold them off. But it scared the Old Man. You see, our competitive position is based on Lani labor. Our competitors didn't know that. Their intelligence wasn't so good. Up until that time, we'd been keeping the males out here in what was hardly more than a stockade. Those people could have taken a few dozen females and a couple of males and they'd have been in business. But they didn't know. They tried to smash Alexandria instead. Naturally they didn't have a chance. And after it was over the Old Man got smart. He still had the tapes for Alexandria so he built a duplicate out here and spent a few millions on modern armament. The way we're set now it'd take a battle group to hurt us."

"But how about security? Don't the others know about the Lani now?"

"It's a moot question. But it won't do them any good. They can't crack this place, and without males, all the females on Flora wouldn't do them enough long-term good to pay for the force they'd need to be successful."

"So that's why the males are isolated."

"There's another reason—two of them in fact. One is physical. Even the best male is a dangerous beast. They have a flair for violence that makes them useless as labor and their training doesn't help matters. And the other is mental. The females on the main island believe that we humans are responsible for the continuation of their breed. This tends to keep them in line. We have a great deal more trouble with them out here once they know the truth. We've had a number of cases of females trying to engineer a male's escape. But they're never repeated," Mullins said grimly. "Actually, it would be an interesting life out here, except for the abattoir." He grimaced. "That's an unpleasant chore."

"You mean——" Kennon said.

"Why, certainly. What else could we do with senile animals?"

"But that's murder!"

Mullins shook his head. "No more than killing a cow for beef."

"You know," Kennon said, "I've never though of what happened to aged Lani. Sure, I've never seen one, but—Lord Lister!—I'm a fool."

"You'll get used to the idea," Mullins said. "They aren't human, and except for a few, they aren't as intelligent as a Santosian Varl. I know that they look like us except for those tails, but that's as far as it goes. I've spent two hundred years with them and I know what I'm talking about."

"That's what Alexander says."

"He should know. He's lived with them all his life."

"Well—perhaps. But I'm not convinced."

"Neither was Old Doc—not until the day he died."

"Did he change then?"

"I don't know. I wasn't there. But Old Doc was a stubborn cuss."

Kennon stood up. "I've given instructions for treatment to your corpsman," he said. "Now I think I'd better be getting back. I have some reports to finish."

Mullins smiled grimly. "You know," he said, "I get the feeling that you don't approve of this operation."

"Frankly, I don't," Kennon said, "but I signed a contract." He turned toward the door and gestured to the two Lani who waited outside with his bags. "I can find my way to the roof," he said.

"Well—good luck," Mullins said. "We'll call you again if we need you."

"Do that," Kennon replied. He wanted to leave, to get away from this place and back to the main island. He wanted to see Copper. He'd be damned if anyone was going to butcher her. If he had to stay here until she died of old age, he'd do it. But nobody was going to hurt her.

CHAPTER XII

Kennon wondered if his colleagues in human medicine felt toward their patients as he did toward the Lani, or if they ultimately lost their individuality and became mere hosts for diseases, parasites, and tumors—vehicles for the practice of surgical and medical skills—economic units whose well-being meant a certain amount of credits. Probably not, he decided. They were human and their very humanity made them persons rather than things.

But the possession of individuality was not an asset in the practice of animal medicine where economics was the main factor and the satisfaction of the owner the principal personality problem. The normal farm animals, the shrakes, cattle, sheep, morks, and swine were no problem. They were merely a job. But the Lani were different. They weren't human, but they were intelligent and they did have personality even though they didn't possess that indefinable quality that separated man from the beasts. It was hard to treat them with dispassionate objectivity. In fact, it was impossible.

And this lack of objectivity annoyed him. Should he be this way? Was he right to identify them as individuals and treat them as persons rather than things? The passing months had failed to rob them of their personalities: they had not become the faceless mass of a herd of cattle or a flock of sheep. They were still not essentially different from humans—and wouldn't men themselves lose many of their human characteristics if they were herded into barracks and treated as property for forty generations? Wouldn't men, too, approach the animal condition if they were bred and treated as beasts, their pedigrees recorded, their types winnowed and selected? The thought was annoying.

It would be better, Kennon reflected, if he didn't have time to think, if he were so busy he could drop to his bed exhausted each night and sleep without dreaming, if he could keep on the run so fast that he wouldn't have time to sit and reflect. But he had done his work too well. He had trained his staff too thoroughly. They could handle the petty routines of minor treatment and laboratory tests as well as he. He had only the intellectual stimulation of atypical cases, and these were all too rare. The routine inspections were boring, yet he forced himself to make them because they filled the time. The hospital wards were virtually empty of patients, the work was up to date, the whole island was enjoying a carnival of health, and Kennon was still impaled upon the horns of his dilemma. It wasn't so bad now that the first shock was over, but it was bad enough—and showed no signs of getting better. Now that Copper realized he wanted her, she did nothing to make his life easier. Instead she did her best to get underfoot, usually in some provocative position. It was enough to try the patience of a marble statue, Kennon reflected grimly. But it did have its humorous side, and were it not for the fact that Copper wasn't human it could have been thoroughly enjoyable. That, however, was the real hell of it. He couldn't relax and enjoy the contest—his feet were on too slippery ground. And Copper with her unerring female instinct knew just what to do to make the footing slipperier. Sooner or later, she was certain that he would fall. It was only a question of applying sufficient pressure at the right spot and the right time. Now that she knew he desired her, she was content to wait. The only thing that had bothered her was the uncertainty whether he cared or not. For Copper the future was a simple thing and she was lighthearted about it. But not so Kennon. Even after the initial shock had passed there still remained the moral customs, the conditioning, and the prohibitions. But Copper—was Copper—and somehow the conditioning lost its force in her presence. Perhaps, he thought wryly, it was a symptom of the gradual erosion of his moral character in this abnormal environment.

"I'm getting stale," he confided to Copper as he sat in his office idly turning the pages of the *Kardon Journal of Allied Medical Sciences*. "There's nothing to do that's interesting."

"You could help me," Copper said as she looked up from the pile of cards she was sorting. He had given her the thankless task of reorganizing the files, and she was barely half through the project.

"There's nothing to do that's interesting," he repeated. He cocked his head to one side. From this angle Copper looked decidedly intriguing as she bent over the file drawer and replaced a stack of cards.

"I could suggest something," Copper said demurely.

"Yes, I know," he said. "You're full of suggestions."

"I was thinking that we could go on a picnic."

"A what?"

"A picnic. Take a lunch and go somewhere in the jeep. Maybe up into the hills. I think it might be fun."

"Why not?" Kennon agreed. "At least it would break the monotony. Tell you what. You run up to the house and tell Kara to pack a lunch and we'll take the day off."

"Good! I hoped you'd say that. I'm getting tired of these dirty old cards." She stood up and sidled past the desk. Kennon resisted the impulse to slap as she went past, and congratulated himself on his self-control as she looked at him with a half-disappointed expression on her face. She had expected it, he thought gleefully. Score one for morality.

He smiled. Whatever the other Lani might be, Copper was different. Quick, volatile, intelligent, she was a constant delight, a flashing kaleidoscope of unexpected facets. Perhaps the others were the same if he knew them better. But he didn't know them—and avoided learning. In that direction lay ulcers.

"We'll go to Olympus," he said.

Copper looked dubious. "I'd rather not go there. That's forbidden ground."

"Oh nonsense. You're merely superstitious."

She smiled. "Perhaps you're right. You usually are."

"That's the virtue of being a man. Even if I'm wrong, I'm right." He chuckled at the peculiar expression on her face. "Now off with you—and get that lunch basket packed."

She bowed. "Yes, master. Your slave flies on winged feet to execute your commands."

Kennon chuckled. Copper had been reading Old Doc's romances again. He recognized the florid style.

Kennon landed the jeep in a mountain meadow halfway up the slope of the peacefully slumbering volcano. It was quiet and cool, and the light breeze was blowing Olympus's smoky cap away from them to the west. Copper unpacked the lunch. She moved slowly. After all, there was plenty of time, and she wasn't very hungry. Neither was Kennon.

"Let's go for a walk," Copper said. "The woods look cool—and maybe we can work up an appetite."

"Good idea. I could use some exercise. That lunch looks big enough to choke a horse and I'd like to do it justice."

They walked through the woods, skirting scant patches of underbrush, slowly moving higher on the mountain slopes. The trees, unlike those of Beta, did not end abruptly at a snow line, but pushed green fingers upward through passages between old lava flows, on whose black wrinkled surfaces nothing grew. The faint hum of insects and the piping calls of the birdlike mammals added to the impression of remoteness. It was hard to believe that scarcely twenty kilometers from this primitive microcosm was the border of the highly organized and productive farmlands of Outworld Enterprises.

"Do you think we can see the hospital if we go high enough?" Copper said. She panted a little, unaccustomed to the altitude.

"Possibly," Kennon said. "It is a long distance away. But we should be able to see Alexandria," he added. "That's high enough and big enough." He looked at her curiously. "How is it that you're so breathless?" he asked. "We're not that high. You're getting fat with too much soft living."

Copper smiled. "Perhaps I'm getting old."

"Nonsense," Kennon chuckled. "It's just fat. Come to think of it you *are* plumper. Not that I mind, but if you're going to keep that sylphlike figure you'd better go on a diet."

"You're too good to me," Copper said.

"You're darn right I am. Well—let's get going. Exercise is always good for the waistline, and I'd like to see what's up ahead."

Scarcely a kilometer ahead they came to a wall of lava that barred their path. "Oh, oh," Kennon said. "We can't go over *that*." He looked at the wrinkled and shattered rock with its knifelike edges.

"I don't think my feet could take it," Copper admitted. "It looks like the end of the trail."

"No—not quite," Kennon said. "There seems to be a path here." He pointed to a narrow cleft in the black rock. "Let's see where it goes."

Copper hung back. "I don't think I want to," she said doubtfully. "It looks awfully dark and narrow."

"Oh, stop it. Nothing's going to hurt us. Come on." Kennon took her hand.

Unwillingly Copper allowed herself to be led forward. "There's something about this place that frightens me," she said uncomfortably as the high black walls closed in, narrowing until only a slit of yellow sky was visible overhead. The path underfoot was surprisingly smooth and free from rocks, but the narrow corridor, steeped in shadows, was gloomy and depressingly silent. It even bothered Kennon, although he wouldn't admit it. What forces had sliced this razor-thin cleft in the dense rock around them? Earthquake probably. And if it happened once it could happen again. He would hate to be trapped here entombed in shattered rock.

Gradually the passage widened, then abruptly it ended. A bleak vista of volcanic ash dotted with sputter cones opened before them. It was a flat tableland, roughly circular, scarcely half a kilometer across, a desolation of black rock, stunted trees and underbrush, and gray volcanic ash. A crater, somewhat larger than the rest, lay with its nearest edge about two hundred meters away. The rock edges were fire polished, gleaming in the yellow sunshine, and the thin margin of trees and brush surrounding the depression were gnarled and shrunken, twisted into fantastic shapes.

"Hey! what's this?" Kennon asked curiously. "That crater looks peculiar, like a meteor had struck here—but those stunted plants—hmm—there must have been some radioactivity too." He looked at the crater speculatively. "Now I wonder——" he began.

Copper had turned a sickly white. "No!" she said in a half-strangled voice—"oh, *no!*"

Kennon looked at her. "You know what this is?" he demanded.

"No," Copper said. But her voice was unsteady.

"You're lying."

"But I *don't* know." Copper wailed. "I'm only guessing. I've never seen this place before in my life! Please!—let's get out of here!"

"Then you know *about* this," Kennon demanded.

"I think it's the Pit," Copper said. "The redes don't say where it is. But the description fits—the Circle of Death, the Twisted Land—it's all like the redes say."

"Redes?—what are redes? And what is this business about circles of death? There's something here that's peculiar and I want to know what it is."

"It's nothing. Truly. Just let's go back. Let's leave this place. It's no good. It's tabu."

"Tabu? You've never used that word before."

"Forbidden."

"Who forbids it?"

"The Gods—the Old Ones. It is not for Lani. Nor for you." Her voice was harsh. "Come away before it is too late. Before the Silent Death strikes you down."

"I'm going to have a look at this."

"You'll be killed!" Copper said. "And if you die, I die too."

"Don't be foolish. There's nothing here that can hurt me. See those trees and plants growing right up to the crater's edge. If they can take it permanently, I can stand it for a few moments. If there's any radioactivity there, it's not very much."

"But the redes say——"

"Oh, forget those redes. I know what I'm doing. Besides, I'm a Betan and can stand more radiation than most men. A brief exposure isn't going to hurt me."

"You go and I go too," Copper said desperately.

"You'll stay here where it's safe," Kennon said flatly.

"I'm going with you," Copper repeated. "I don't want to live without you."

"I tell you I won't be hurt. And one quick look isn't going to bother whatever's down there."

"That's what Roga the Foolish said when he opened Lyssa's tower. But he brought men to Flora. And your little look may bring an even greater calamity."

Kennon shrugged, and started walking toward the crater's edge.

Copper followed.

He turned to order her back, but the words died on his lips as he saw the terror and determination on her face. Neither commands nor pleas would move her. If he went she would follow. The only way he could stop her would be with violence, and he didn't want to manhandle her. He felt an odd mixture of pride, tenderness, and admiration for her. Were their situations reversed, he doubted whether he would have the courage she was showing. He sighed. Perhaps she was right. Perhaps he did need an antiradiation suit.

"All right," he said. "You win. I'll get some protective clothing and look at it later."

Her knees sagged, but he caught her before she fell, and held her erect until her strength returned. Belatedly he understood the emotional strain that had been gripping her. "If you come back later, sir, you'll take me with you." The words were a statement, not a question.

He nodded. "Providing you wear a radiation suit," he said.

She grimaced with distaste and he chuckled. Clothing and Copper simply didn't get along together.

"Well?"

"All right," she said unhappily.

"And there's one more condition."

"What's that?" she asked suspiciously.

"That you tell me about this place. You obviously know something about it, and with all your talking, you've never mentioned it to me."

"It is forbidden to talk of these things to men," Copper said—and then, perversely, "Do you want me to tell you now?"

"No—it can wait. We have come a long way and I am hungry. I listen poorly on an empty stomach. Let's go back to the jeep and you can tell me later."

Copper smiled. "That's good," she said. "I'd feel better away from this place."

CHAPTER XIII

"I was a poor learner of the redes," Copper confessed. "And I'll have to skip the Mysteries. I never even tried to learn them. Somehow I was sure I'd never be a preceptress." She settled herself more comfortably on the tawny grass and watched him as he lay on his back beside her.

"Eh?" Kennon said, "Preceptress?"

"The guardians of our traditions. They know the redes and mysteries by heart."

"And you have kept your religion alive that way all these years?"

"It isn't exactly religion," Copper said. "It's more like history, we learn it to remember that we were once a great race—and that we may be again. Someday there will come a male, a leader to bring us out of bondage, and our race will be free of dependence on men. There will be pairings again, and freedom to live as we please." She looked thoughtfully at Kennon. "You might even be the one—even though you are human. You're different from the others."

"You're prejudiced." Kennon smiled. "I'm no different. Well—not very different at any rate."

"That is not my thought," Copper said. "You are very different indeed. No man has ever resisted a Lani as long as you have."

Kennon shook his head. "Let's not go into that now. What are these redes?"

"I do not remember them all," Copper apologized. "I was——"

"You've said that before. Tell me what you *do* know."

"I remember the beginning fairly well," she said. "It goes back to the time before Flora when everything was nothing and the Master Himself was lonely."

Without warning her voice changed to a rhythmic, cadenced chant that was almost a song. Her face became rapt and introspective as she rocked slowly from side to side. The rhythm was familiar and then he recognized it—the unintelligible music he had often heard coming from the barracks late at night when no men were around—the voiceless humming that the Lani sang at work.

> First there was Darkness—starless and sunless
> Void without form—darker than night
> Then did the Master—Lord of Creation
> Wave His right hand, saying, "Let there be light!"

Verse, Kennon thought. That was logical. People remember poetry better than prose. But the form was not what he'd normally expect. It was advanced, a style that was past primitive blank verse or heroic pentameter. He listened intently as Copper went on.

> Light filled the heavens, bright golden glowing,
> Brought to the Void by His wondrous hand;
> Then did the Master—Lord of Creation—
> Nod His great head, saying, "Let there be land!"
>
> Air, land, and water formed into being,
> Born in the sight of His all-seeing eyes;
> Then did the master—Lord of Creation—
> Smile as He murmured, "Let life arise!"
>
> All of the life conceived by the Master,
> Varied in shape as the grasses and birds;
> Hunters and hunted, moveless and moving,
> Came into form at the sound of His words.

"That's a great deal like Genesis," Kennon said with mild astonishment. "Where could you have picked that up?"

"From the beginning of our race," Copper said. "It came to us with Ulf and Lyssa—but what is Genesis?"

"A part of an ancient religion—one that is still followed on some of the Central Worlds. Its followers call themselves Christians. They say it came from Earth, the motherworld of men."

"*Our* faith has no name. We are children of Lyssa, who was a daughter of the Master."

"It is an odd similarity," Kennon said. "But other races have had stories of the Creation. And possibly there may be another explanation. Your ancestors could have picked this up from Alexander's men. They came from Earth originally and some of them could have been Christians."

"No," Cooper said. "This rede is long before Man Alexander. It is the origin of our world, even before Ulf and Lyssa. It is the first Book—the Book of the God-spell. Man Alexander came in the sixth Book—the Book of Roga."

"There's no point in arguing about it," Kennon said. "Go on—tell me the rest."

"It's going to be a long story," Copper said. "Even though I have forgotten some of it, I can chant the redes for hours."

Kennon braced his back against one of the fat tires of the jeep. "I'm a good listener," he said.

She chuckled. "You asked for this," she said—and took up the verses where she had left off. And Kennon learned the Lani version of creation, of the first man and woman, cast out of Heaven for loving each other despite the Master's objection, of how they came to Flora and founded the race of the Lani. He learned how the Lani grew in numbers and power, how they split into two warring groups over the theological point of whether Ulf or Lyssa was the principal deity, how Roga the Foolish opened Lyssa's tower to find out whether the Ulfians or Lyssans were right, and brought the Black Years to Flora.

He heard the trial of Roga and the details of his torture by the priests of Ulf and the priests of Lyssa—united by this greatest sacrilege. And he heard the Lani version of the landing of Alexander's ship and man's conquest of Flora.

It was a story of savagery and superstition, of blood and intolerance, of bravery and cowardice, of love and beauty. Yet through it all, even through the redes that described the Conquest, there was a curious remoteness, a lack of emotion that made the verses more terrible as they flowed in passionless rhythm from Copper's lips.

"That's enough!" Kennon said.

"I told you you wouldn't like it."

"It's horrible. How can you remember such things?"

"We begin to learn them as soon as we can talk. We know the redes almost our entire lives." Copper was silent for a moment. "There's lots more," she said, "but it's all about our lives since the Man Alexander—the old one—took possession of us. And most of the newer redes are pretty dull. Our life hasn't changed much since the men came. The Book of Man is boring." Copper sighed. "I have dared a great deal by telling you these things. If the others knew, they would kill both of us."

"Then why tell me?" he asked.

"I love you," she said simply. "You wanted to know—and I can deny you nothing."

A wave of tenderness swept over him. She would give her life for him—and what would he give? Nothing. Not even his prejudices. His face twisted. If she was only human. If she wasn't just an animal. If he wasn't a Betan. If, if, if. Resentment gorged his throat. It was unfair—so damned unfair. He had no business coming here. He should have stayed on Beta or at least on a human world where he

85

would never have met Copper. He loved her, but he couldn't have her. It was Tantalus and Sisyphus rolled into one unsightly package and fastened to his soul. With a muttered curse he rose to his feet, and as he did he stopped—frozen—staring at Copper as though he had never seen her before.

"*How* did you say that Roga was judged responsible for Alexander coming here?" he demanded.

"He went into Lyssa's tower—where Ulf and Lyssa tried to call Heaven—and with his foolish meddling set the tower alight with a glow that all could see. Less than a week later the Man Alexander came."

"Where was this tower?"

"Where Alexandria now stands. Man Alexander destroyed it and built his house upon its ruins."

"And what was that place of the Pit?"

"The Shrine of Ulf—where the God-Egg struck Flora. It is buried in the pit, but the Silent Death has protected it from blasphemy—and besides Man Alexander never learned about it. We feared that he would destroy it as he did Lyssa's tower.'"

A wild hope stirred in Kennon. "We're going home," he announced.

"Good."

"And we're going to get a pair of radiation suits—and then we're coming back. We'll have a good look at that Pit, and if what's in there is what I think it is"—his face was a mixture of grimness and eagerness—"we'll blow this whole operation off this planet!"

Copper blanched. "It is death to meddle with the God-Egg," she said.

"Superstition!" Kennon scoffed. "If that Egg is what I think, it was made by men, and you are their descendant."

"Perhaps you're right, but I can't help thinking you are wrong," she said soberly. "Look at the trouble that came with Roga's meddling. Be careful that you do not bring us a worse fate."

"I'll be very careful. We'll take every precaution."

"We?"

"You're coming, of course. I can't imagine you staying away."

Copper nodded.

"You shouldn't worry so much," Kennon teased. "You know we men live forever."

"That is true."

"And if I'm right you're just as human as I. And you're capable of living as long as I do."

"Yes, sir," Copper said. Her voice was unconvinced, her expression noncommittal.

"You females," Kennon said in quick exasperation. "You drive a man crazy. Get an idea in your head and it takes triatomate to blast it out. Now let's go."

Two hours brought them back to the volcanic area, and knowing what to look for, Kennon located the pockmarked mountain valley. From the air it looked completely ordinary. Kennon was amazed at the perfection of the natural camouflage. The Pit was merely another crater in the pitted ground. He dropped to a lower altitude, barely a hundred feet above the sputter cones. "Look!" he said.

Below them was the crater of the Pit and in its center a smooth bluish-black hemisphere protruded from the crater floor. It would have passed unnoticed by the casual eye— nearly concealed by two gigantic blocks of pumice.

"The God-Egg!" Copper exlaimed.

"Egg—ha! that's a spacer! I thought it would be. I'd recognize durilium anywhere. Let's go down and look this over, but first we want a couple of pictures." He pointed a camera at the crater and snapped the shutter. "There—now let's have a closer look at our baby."

"Do you expect me to get into that thing?" Copper said distastefully as she prodded the shapeless green coveralls with a bare toe. She eyed the helmet, gloves and boots with equal distaste. "I'd suffocate."

"If you want to come with me you'll wear it," Kennon said. "Otherwise you won't come near that pit. Try it and I'll chain you to the jeep."

"You wouldn't!"

"Just try me."

"Oh—all right. I'll wear the thing—but I won't be comfortable."

"Who cares about that? You'll be protected."

"All right—show me how to put it on. I'd rather be with you than worry about what you are doing."

The suit was several sizes too large but it covered her adequately. Too adequately, Kennon decided. She looked like a pile of wrinkles with legs. He chuckled.

She glared. "So I'm funny," she said. "Let me tell you something else that's funny. I'm hot. I'm sweating. I itch. Now—laugh!"

"I don't feel like laughing," Kennon said. "I feel the same way."

They approached the edge of the Pit carefully. Kennon kept checking the radiation counter. The needle slowly rose and steadied at one-half roentgen per hour as he thrust the probe over the rim of the depression. "It's fine, so far," he said encouragingly. "We could take this much for quite a while even without suits." He lowered himself over the edge, sliding down the gentle slope.

"How is it down there?" Copper called. The intercom crackled in his ear.

"Fine—barely over one roentgen per hour. With these suits we could stay here indefinitely." The sigh of relief was music in her ears. "This place is barely lukewarm."

"That's what you think," Copper said.

"I mean radiation warm," Kennon said. "Stay up there and watch me. I may need some things."

"All right." Copper squirmed inside the hot suit. The thing was an oven. She hoped that Kennon didn't plan to work in the daytime. It would be impossible.

Kennon gingerly approached the ship. It was half buried in the loose debris and ash that had fallen or blown into the pit during the centuries it had rested there. It was old—incredibly old. The hull design was ancient—riveted sheets of millimeter-thick durilium. Ships hadn't been built like that in over two thousand years. And the ovoid shape was reminiscent of the even more ancient spindizzy design. A hyperspace converter like that couldn't be less than four millennia old. It was a museum piece, but the blue-black hull was as smooth and unblemished as the day it had left fabrication.

Space travel would have gotten nowhere without durilium, Kennon reflected. For five thousand years men had used the incredibly tough synthetic to build their spacecraft. It had given man his empire. Kennon gave the hull one quick glance. That part of the ship didn't worry him. It was what he would find inside that bothered him. How much damage had occurred from two thousand or more years of disuse? How much had the original travelers cannibalized? How much could be salvaged? What sort of records remained? There were a thousand questions that the interior of that enigmatic hull might answer.

The upper segment of the airlock was visible. It was closed, which was a good sign. A few hours' work with a digger should expose it enough to be opened.

"Copper," he said, "we're going to have to dig this out. There's a small excavator in the cargo bed of the jeep. Do you think you can bring it down here?"

"I think so."

"Good girl!" Kennon turned back to the ship. He was

eager to enter it. There might be things inside that would settle the question of the Lani. The original crew had probably recognized the value of the hull as a repository as well as he did. But in the meantime there would be work —lots of it. And every step must be recorded.

It was the rest of the day's work to expose the emergency airlock. The little excavator toiled over the loose ash for hours before it displaced enough to make the port visible, and the ash was not yet cleared away sufficiently to open the portal when darkness brought a halt to the work.

It would be impossible to unearth the spaceship with their low-capacity digger, Kennon decided. It would be difficult enough to clear the emergency airlock in the nose. But if the tubes and drive were still all right, by careful handling it should be possible to use the drive to blast out the loose ash and cinders which surrounded the hull.

Kennon reluctantly gave up the idea of entering the spaceship. That would have to wait until tomorrow. Now they would have to conceal the work and call it a day. A few branches and the big blocks of pumice would suffice for temporary camouflage. Later they could make something better. Anything in the jeep which might be useful was cached along with the radiation suits in the passageway through the lava wall—and in a surprisingly short time they were heading homeward.

Kennon was not too displeased. Tomorrow they would be able to enter the ship. Tomorrow they would probably have some of the answers to his questions. He looked ahead into the gathering night. The gray mass of the abandoned Olympus Station slipped below them as he lined the jeep along the path indicated by the luminous arrow atop the main building, set the controls on automatic, and locked the craft on the guide beacon in Alexandria's tower. In a little less than an hour they would be home.

CHAPTER XIV

Kennon was morally certain that the Lani were of human stock. Evolved, of course. Mutated. Genetic strangers to the rest of humanity. But human. The spaceship and the redes proved it as far as he was concerned. But moral certainty and legal certainty were two different things. What he believed might be good enough to hold up in a Brotherhood court, but he doubted it. Ulf and Lyssa might be the founders of the Lani race, but they had come to Kardon nearly four thousand years ago and no records existed to prove that the Lani weren't here before they came. Redes passed by word of mouth through hundreds of generations were not evidence. Even the spaceship wasn't the absolute proof that would be needed to overturn the earlier legal decision. Other and better proof was needed—something that would stand up in any court in the Brotherhood. He hoped the spaceship would hold that proof.

But Kennon's eagerness to find out what was inside the ancient spacer was tempered by hard practicality. Too much depended on what he might find inside that hull. Every step of the work must be documented beyond any refutation. Some method of establishing date, time, and location had to be prepared. There must be a record of every action. And that would require equipment and planning. There must be no mistake that could be twisted by the skillful counsel that Alexander undoubtedly retained.

He had no doubt that the Family would fight. Too much money and prestige were involved. To prove the Lani human would destroy Outworld Enterprises on Kardon. Yet this thought did not bother him. To his surprise he had no qualms of conscience. He was perfectly willing to violate his contract, break faith with his employers, and plot their ruin. The higher duty came first—the duty to the human race.

He smiled wryly. It wasn't all higher duty. There were some personal desires that leavened the nobility. To prove Copper human was enough motivation—actually it was better than his sense of duty. Events, Kennon reflected, cause a great deal of change in one's attitude. Although not by nature a plotter, schemes had been flitting through his mind with machinelike regularity, to be examined and discarded, or to be set aside for future reference.

He rejected the direct approach. It was too dangerous, depended too much on personalities, and had too little chance for success. He considered the possibility of letters to the Brotherhood Council but ultimately rejected it. Not only was the proof legally insufficient to establish humanity in the Lani, but he also remembered Alexander's incredible knowledge of his activities, and there was no reason to suppose that his present didn't receive the same scrutiny as the past. And if he, who hadn't written a letter in over a year, suddenly began to write, the correspondence would undoubtedly be regarded with suspicion and would probably be examined, and Dirac messages would be out for the same reason.

He could take a vacation and while he was away from the island he could inform the Brotherhood. Leaving Flora wouldn't be particularly difficult, but leaving Kardon would be virtually impossible. His contract called for vacations, but it expressly provided that they would be taken on Kardon. And again, there would be no assurance that his activities would not be watched. In fact, it was probable that they would be.

There was nothing that could be done immediately. But there were certain long-range measures that could be started. He could begin preparing a case that could be presented to the Council. And Beta, when it knew, would help him. The situation of the Lani was so close to Beta's own that its obvious merit as a test case simply could not be ignored. If he could get the evidence to Beta, it would be easy to enlist the aid of the entire Medico-Technological Civilization. It would take time and attention to detail; the case, the evidence, everything would have to be prepared with every safeguard and contingency provided, so that there would not be the slightest chance of a slip-up once it came to court.

And perhaps the best method of bringing the evidence would be to transport it under its own power. The thought intrigued him. Actually it wouldn't be too difficult. Externally the Egg wasn't in bad shape. The virtually indestructible durilium hull was still intact. The controls and the engines, hermetically sealed inside the hull, were probably as good as the day they stopped running. The circuitry would undoubtedly be bad but it could be repaired and restored, and new fuel slugs could be obtained for the engine and the converter. But that was a problem for the future.

The immediate problem was to get into the ship in a properly documented fashion.

It took nearly two months, but finally, under the impersonal lenses of cameras and recorders, the entrance port of the God-Egg swung open and revealed the dark interior. Kennon moved carefully, recording every step as he entered the black orifice in the spaceship's side. His handtorch gave plenty of light for the recorders as he moved inside—

Copper at his heels, both of them physically unrecognizable in antiradiation suits.

"Why are we moving so slowly?" Copper said. "Let's go ahead and find out what's beyond this passageway."

"From a superstitious coward you've certainly become a reckless explorer," he said.

"The Egg hasn't hurt us, and we've been around it many times," she said. "Either the curse has become too old to hurt us, or there never was any in the first place. So let's see what is ahead. I'm curious."

Kennon shook his head. "In this business we must hurry slowly—very slowly. You know why."

"But I want to see."

"Patience, girl. Simmer down. You'll see soon enough," Kennon said. "Now help me set up this camera."

"Oh, all right—but isn't there any excitement in you?"

"I'm bubbling over with it," Kennon admitted, "but I manage to keep it under control."

"You're cold-blooded."

"No—I'm sensible. We want to nail this down. My future, yours, and that of your people depend upon how carefully we work. You wouldn't want to let us all down by being too eager, would you?"

She shook her head. "No—you're right of course. But I still would like to see."

They moved cautiously through the airlock and into the control room.

"Ah!" Kennon said with satisfaction. "I hoped for this, but I didn't dare expect it."

"What?"

"Look around. What do you see?"

"Nothing but an empty room. It's shaped like half an orange, and it has a lot of funny instruments and dials on the walls, and a video screen overhead. But that's all. Why —what's so unusual about it? It looks just like someone had left it."

"That's the point. There's nothing essential that's missing. They didn't cannibalize the instruments—and they didn't come back."

"Why not?"

"Maybe because that curse you mentioned a few minutes ago was real."

Copper drew back. "But you said it wouldn't hurt us——"

"Not now. The heat's practically gone, but when whoever flew this crate came here, the whole shell could have been as hot as a Samarian summer."

"But couldn't they have come back when it cooled?"

"Not with this kind of heat. The hull was probably too radioactive to approach from the outside. And radioactivity cools off slowly. It might take several lifetimes for its level to become low enough to approach if there was no decontamination equipment available."

"I suppose that's why the early ones thought the Egg was cursed."

Kennon nodded. "Now let's check—oh! oh! what's this?" He pointed to a metal-backed book lying on the control panel.

"It looks like a book," Copper said.

"I'm hoping it's *the* book."

"The book?"

"Yes—the ship's log. It's possible. And if it is, we may have all the evidence we need—Copper!—*Don't touch it!*"

"Why not?"

"Because its position has to be recorded first. Wait until we get the camera and recorders set up."

Gingerly Kennon opened the ancient book. The sheets inside were brittle—crumbling with age—but he could make out the title *U.N.S.S. Wanderer* with the date of launching and a lower line which read "Ship's Log." Kennon was thankful for his medical training. The four years of Classical English that he had despised so much were essential now. Stumbling over unfamiliar words and phrases, he moved slowly through the log tracing the old ship's history from pleasure craft to short-haul freight tractor to obsolescence in a space dump orbiting around a world called Heaven.

There was a gap of nearly ten years indicated by a blank page before the entries resumed.

"Ah—this is it!" Kennon said.

"What is it?" Copper said curiously. "I can't read the writing."

"Of course you can't. It's in English—a language that became obsolete during the Interregnum. I had to learn it, since most medical terminology is based on it."

"What is an Interregnum?" Copper interrupted. "I've never heard that word before."

"It's a period of confusion when there is no stable government. The last one came after the Second Galactic War—but never mind that—it happened long ago and isn't important now. The important thing that did happen was the Exodus."

"What was that?"

"A religious revival and a tremendous desire to see what was happening beyond the next star. During that century men traveled wider and farther then they ever have before or since. In that outward explosion with its mixed motivations of religion and practicality, colonists and missionaries went starward to find new worlds to tame, and new races to be rescued from the darkness of idolatry and hell. Almost any sort of vehicle capable of mounting a spindizzy converter was pressed into service. The old spindizzies were soundly engineered converters of almost childlike simplicity that could and did carry ships enormous distances if their passengers didn't care about subjective time-lag, and a little radioactivity.

"And that's what happened to this ship. According to this log it was bought by Alfred and Melissa Weygand— a missionary couple with the idea of spreading the Christian faith to the heathen.

"Alfred and Melissa—Ulf and Lyssa—they were a part of this ancient explosion that scattered human seed across parsecs of interstellar space. It seems that they were a unit in a missionary fleet that had gone out to the stars with flame in their hearts and Gospel on their lips to bring the Word to the benighted heathen on other worlds." Kennon's lips curled with mild contempt at their stupid foolhardiness even as his pulse quickened to their bravery. They had been fanatics, true enough, but theirs was a selfless fanaticism that would risk torture and death for what they believed—a fanaticism that was more sublime than the concept of Brotherhood which had evolved from it. They knew nothing of the enmity of race, of the incessant struggle man had since waged with alien intelligences all too willing to destroy intruders who encroached upon their worlds. Mankind's early selflessness had long ago been discarded for frank expansionism and dominance over the lesser races that stood in their way. And in a way it was too bad.

The ship's log, meticulously kept in neat round English script, told a story that was more than the bare bones of flight. There was passion and tenderness and a spiritual quality that was shocking to a modern man steeped in millennia of conquest and self-interest. There was a greatness to it, a depth of faith that had since been lost. And as Kennon slowly deciphered the ancient script he admired the courage even as his mind winced with dismay at the unheeding recklessness.

The Weygands had lost contact with the others, and had searched for them in hyperspace, doubling and twisting upon their course until they had become hopelessly lost, and then, with their fuel nearly exhausted, had broken out into the normal three-space continuum to find Kardon's sun and the world they called Flora.

How little they had known and how lucky they had been.

It was only by the grace of their God that they had found this world before their fuel was exhausted. And it was only by further grace that the planet was habitable and not populated with intelligent life. They had more luck than people were entitled to in a dozen lifetimes. Against odds of a million to one they had survived.

It was fascinating reading.

But it was not proof.

The last entry read: "We have circled this world and have seen no buildings—no sign of intelligent life. We are lost, marooned on this empty world. Our fuel supplies are too low for us to attempt to find the others. Nor could we. The constellations in the sky are strange. We do not know which way to go. Therefore we shall land upon the great island in the center of the yellow sea. And perhaps someday men will come to us since we cannot return to them. Melissa thinks that this is an example of Divine Providence, that the Lord's mercy has been shown to us that were lost in the vastness of the deep—that we have been chosen, like Eve and Adam, to spread the seed of man to yet another world. I hope she is right, yet I fear the radiation level of the ship has become inordinately high. We may well be Eve and Adam, yet an Adam that cannot beget and an Eve that is not fruitful. I am trimming the ship for landing, and we shall leave it immediately after we have landed, taking with us only what we absolutely need. There is too much radiation from the spindizzy and the drive to remain here longer—and God knows how hot the outer hull may be."

And that was all. Presumptive evidence—yes. Reasonable certainty—yes. But not proof. Lawyers could argue that since no direct exploration was made there was no valid reason to assume that the Lani did not already inhabit Kardon. But Kennon knew. His body, more perceptive than his mind, had realized a truth that his brain would not accept until he read the log. It was at once joy and frustration. Joy that Copper was human, frustration that he could not obtain for her and her race the rights to which they were entitled. But the immediate problem was solved. His conditioning was broken now he was convinced that Copper was a member of the human race. It was no violation of his code to love her. The greatest barrier was broken, and with it gone the lesser ones would yield. Relief that was almost pain washed through him and left him weak with reaction.

"What is it?" Copper asked as he turned to her. "What is this thing that has turned your face to joy?"

"Can't you guess?"

She shook her head. "I have seen nothing but you reading this ancient book, yet you turn to me with the look in your eyes that the redes say Ulf had for Lyssa."

"You're human!"

Copper shrugged. "You're mad. I'm a Lani. I was born a Lani—and I shall die one."

"Don't you understand? All Lani are human. You all are the descendants of two humans who came here thousands of years ago."

"Then there is no reason why you cannot love me."

Kennon shook his head. "No," he said. "There is no reason."

Copper laughed. It was a sound so merry and gay that Kennon looked at her in surprise. She looked as happy as she sounded.

Simple and savage, Kennon thought. She cared nothing for the future, and probably very little about the injustice of her present. The thing that mattered was that what had kept them apart was gone. She was probably offering mental sacrifices to the Old Ones who had caused this change in the man she loved. She didn't really care about what had caused the change. To her it was sufficient that it had happened.

For a moment Kennon wished that it could be as simple for him as it apparently was for her. The fact that Copper was human posed a greater problem than the one it solved. The one had been personal. The other was infinitely greater. He could not let it lie. The very morality which had kept him from doing what he wished when he thought she was a humanoid now forced him to do what he did not wish. Every instinct said to leave it alone. The problem was too great for one man to solve, the situation too complicated, the evidence too inconclusive, the opposition too powerful. It would be far better to take his happiness and enjoy it. It was not his problem to solve. He could turn the evidence over to the Brotherhood once his contract was over, and better and more capable people than he could settle the Lani legal status. But the inner voice that had called him bestial now called him shirker, coward, and slacker. And this, too, could not be borne. The case of the Lani would have to be pursued as vigorously as he could do it. They were entitled to human rights—whether they wanted them or not.

His first idea of making the spacer operational was a good one, Kennon decided as they finished the inspection of the ship. Even if it was never used it would make a good means of retreat. He grinned wryly. In a guerrilla operation such as the one he was considering it would be wise to have a way out if things got too hot. The heavy parts, the engines and the controls, were in workable condition and would merely require cleaning and oiling. Some of the optical equipment would have to be replaced and fuel slugs would have to be obtained for the drive—but none of these would be too hard to accomplish. The slugs from any of the power reactors on the island would serve nicely. All that would have to be done would be to modify the fuel ports on the ship's engine. The spindizzy would have to be disassembled and checked, and the main leads, embedded in time-resistant plastic, would have to be examined. The most serious problem, however, wouldn't involve these things. The control board wiring and circuitry was where the trouble would lie. Normal insulation and printed circuitry wasn't designed to last for thousands of years. Each wired circuit would have to be removed, duplicated, and replaced. Every printed panel would have to be cleaned and receive a new coat of insulating varnish. Working full time, a four-man electronics team could do the job in a week. Working part-time the two of them might get it done in three months. And the other jobs would take at least another. Add a month for errors in judgment, lack of materials, and mistakes—and another for unavoidable delays—it would be at least six months before the Egg would be spaceworthy.

Six months.

Not too long if everything went well, but far too long if there were any mistakes. He would have to be careful, yet he must not give the impression of being careful. He shook his head. Being a subversive was going to require a greater amount of acting ability than he had ever been called upon to display.

And what of Copper? How would she behave under the double strain of knowledge that she was human and knowledge of the spaceship? Women weren't noted for their tight-lipped reticence. Would she tell the other Lani? Would she crack under the pressure? Did she have the qualities of a good conspirator?

As it turned out, he didn't need to worry. As a partner in

crime, Copper was all that could be wished. Everything was normal. She was still obedient, helpful, and gay as ever. To watch her, no one would ever think that her bright head was full of knowledge that could rock Flora to its foundations. Never by look or word did she betray the slightest trace of strain or guilt.

And in her other moments she was ecstatic in her love and helpful with the repair work on the Egg whenever Kennon could get time to visit the old spaceship.

"You amaze me," Kennon said as they eased the cover of the spindizzy in place and spun the bolts on the lugs that held it to the outer shielding. He picked up a heavy wrench and began methodically to seat the bolts as Copper wiped the white extrusion of the cover sealant from the shining case.

"How?"

"The way you hide your knowledge of this ship from the others. I know you better than anyone else on this island, and yet you would fool me."

"We Lani are used to hiding things. You men have been our masters for centuries, yet you do not know our redes. Nor do you know what we think. We obey you, but there are parts of us you do not own. It is easy to hide a little thing like this."

Kennon nodded. It figured. He seated another bolt. Three more and the drive room would be restored and they could start on the control circuits. "I wish you were as clever about adopting human customs as you are about hiding guilty knowledge," he said.

Copper laughed. "You mean those silly things you have been teaching me? Why should I learn them? I'm happy as I am. I love you, you love me, and that is all that matters."

"It's not all that matters. Can't you get it through your head that civilized customs are necessary in a civilized society?" He gave the next-to-last bolt an extra-vicious wrench. "You'll have to know them if you expect to get along on Beta."

"But I will never see Beta."

"I am going there when my duty here is over. And you're going with me."

"When will that be?"

"Three years."

"So long? Well—we can think of it then, but I don't think Man Alexander will let you take me."

"Then I shall take you without his consent."

She smiled. "It would be easier to stay here. In another fifteen years I will be old and you will not want me."

"I'll never do that. I'll always want you."

"You swear too easily," she said gently. "You men live forever. We Lani are a short-lived race."

"But you needn't be. It's obviously——"

"It's been tried, my love—and those who were treated died. Man Alexander tried many years ago to make us long-lived like you. But he failed. You see, he loved one of us too."

"But——"

"Let us think no more of it. Let us enjoy what we have and be grateful to the Gods for the love we enjoy—or do you have any Gods?"

"One."

"Two are better. More, anyway. And besides, Ulf and Lyssa and the God-Egg are responsible for our joy."

"They are indeed," Kennon said.

"Then why should you think of leaving the place where they rule? You should stay here. There will be other Lani when I am gone. You will be happy always."

"Not without you," Kennon said. "Don't you understand that I love you?"

"And I you. But I am a Lani. You are a man."

"You're as human as I am," Kennon said abruptly.

"That is what you say," Copper replied. "I am not so sure. I need more proof than this." She waved her hand at the ship.

"What proof do you need?"

"The same as the proof you men require. If I should have your child, then I would believe that I was human."

"I've told you a thousand times that the radiation on this ship must have affected Ulf and Lyssa's germ plasm. Can't you understand that?"

"I can understand it all right, but it does not change things. Ulf and Lyssa may have been human before they came here, but they were not when they landed. They were Lani, and their children were Lani."

"But they were of human stock."

"The law that lets men become our masters does not agree with you."

"Then the law is wrong. It should be changed."

Copper shrugged. "Two people cannot change a law."

"They can try—particularly if the law is unjust."

Copper sighed. "Is it not enough for us to love? Must you try to run through a wall?"

"When the wall stands in the way of right and justice I must."

Copper looked at him with pity in her green eyes. "This I do not understand. I know nothing of right and justice. What are these things? Just words. Yet you will endanger our happiness for them. If it is my happiness you wish—then leave this foolishness alone. I have fifteen years I can live with you before I am old and you tire of me. With those years I can be content."

"But I can't," Kennon said. "Call me selfish if you wish, but I want you with me as long as I live. I don't want to live my life without you."

"You want too much," Copper said softly. "But if it makes you happy to try to get it, I shall help. And if we do not succeed you will at least be happier for trying. And if you are happy"—she shrugged—"then the rest makes little difference."

That was the crux of the matter, Kennon reflected bitterly. He was convinced she was human. She was not. And until her mind could be changed on that point she would help him but her heart wouldn't be in it. And the only thing that would convince her that she was human would be a child—a child of his begetting. He could perhaps trick her with an artificial insemination of Lani sperm. There were drugs that could suspend consciousness, hypnotics that would make her believe anything she was told while under their influence.

But in the end it would do no good. All witnesses in Brotherhood court actions were examined under psychoprobe, and a hypnotic was of no value against a lie detector that could extract the deepest buried truth. And he would be examined too. The truth would out—and nothing would be gained. In fact—everything would be lost. The attempt at trickery would prejudice any court against the honest evidence they had so painfully collected.

He sighed. The only thing to do was to go on as they were—and hope that the evidence would hold. With Betan legal talent at their back it might. And, of course, they could try to produce a child as nature had intended. They could try—but Kennon knew it would not succeed. It never had.

CHAPTER XV

Copper had been acting strangely of late, Kennon thought as he rolled over in his bed and watched her standing before the full-length mirror on the bathroom door. She pivoted slowly before the glass, eying herself critically, raising her arms over her head, holding them at her sides, flexing her supple spine and tightening muscles that moved like silken cords beneath her golden skin.

"What are you trying to do—become a muscle dancer?" Kennon asked idly.

She whirled, a crimson blush deepening the tan of her face. "You were supposed to be asleep," she said.

"I'm an unregenerate heel," he replied, "and I don't sleep too well nowadays unless you're beside me."

"Well—I suppose you might as well know now as later," she said. "You'll know in any event."

"Know what?"

"That you're right. I am human."

"And what brought on this sudden change of——" He stopped abruptly, his eyes widening.

"Yes," Copper said. "I am with child. Your child."

"But that's impossible."

She shook her head. "It's a miracle perhaps, but it's not impossible. It's happened. Can't you see the difference?"

"See what? You look just as you always do."

"I suppose you can't see it yet," she admitted. "But I am with child. I'm two weeks past my time."

Kennon's mind leaped to the obvious conclusion. Pseudopregnancy. He had seen it before among Lani at Hillside Farm. It was an odd syndrome which occasionally occurred in humans and animals. The brain, desiring children, made demands upon the body and the body responded to its desire by tricking the brain. Lani were fairly subject to it, probably because they had better imaginations. He would run a few tests when they went down to the hospital, and once she realized the practical joke her body was playing everything would be all right. No wonder she seemed excited.

"We'll find out about that later," he said equably. "We'll settle this when we get back to the hospital."

Copper smiled confidently and patted her stomach. "I know what you are thinking, but you're wrong. We Lani know about these things. In forty generations I am the first to conceive as the Master intended."

"I hope you haven't," Kennon said with such bitter sincerity that Copper looked at him wide-eyed. "Not now. Because if you have, neither your life nor mine is safe."

"Why?"

"The Alexanders. Do you think they'll take it lying down? We're not ready for them yet. They'll fight, and the first thing they'll do is kill you and erase me so we would never be able to talk. You have been declared an animal, and you will not be allowed to change."

"What can we do?" Copper asked. She shivered. "I do not want to die."

"Nor do I want you to," Kennon said.

"I could tell the others."

"And just what would that accomplish?"

"In a week every Lani on the island would know it. There would be revolt. For the Lani would no longer be dependent upon Men to survive. Their greatest hold on us would be gone. And we would be free again on our island world."

"You would *not!*" Kennon said. "That sort of thinking is foolishness. Alexander would have men here within a week, and a week after that you would be smashed. Don't you realize that there are thousands of millions of men in the galaxy—and to every one of them you would be animals. You know nothing about what you would face. Your puny hundreds couldn't even stand against a fraction of the power Alexander could mount against you. Have you seen a Burkholtz blaster work? Have you seen remote-control antipersonnel missiles? Have you push-pull projectors, atomic warheads? All of these weapons Alexander can command. Don't you realize he's an entrepreneur?—one of the most powerful men in this sector?"

Copper shook her head. "No," she said in a small voice. "I know nothing about these things."

"And do you think forty generations of absolute obedience to men can be overcome because one Lani says she is pregnant by a man?"

Copper frowned. "You put that in a different way. You talk as if it were my belief rather than the truth."

"What is truth?" Kennon said heavily. "Who would believe you? There are hundreds of others with child.

"Sure you're human. You know it. I know it. I've been trying to convince you for the past two months. You're just as human as I am. But pray that you're not pregnant. We can't get out of here in less than four months and by then everybody will know about you. Someone will certainly check the records. And after that will come the psychoprobes. Everything will come to light. The Egg will be destroyed. I will be erased. You will be dead. And that will be the end of it." He looked down at her with an odd expression of pity on his face. "You see?" he demanded harshly.

Copper nodded. "I didn't understand," she said. "Don't be angry with me. I shouldn't have told you. I thought you'd be happy."

"I was never angry with you, but I am with myself. I was stupid. I didn't figure on the remote possibility that we might be genetically compatible. I should have my head examined for putting you in such danger. However there's the possibility—the probability—that your body is playing a trick upon you."

She shook her head. "You are wrong. I am not mistaken. I am with child and the child is yours. But the fault is no more yours than mine. I wanted you before you looked on me. I still do and I do not feel at fault. That I am yours, that my child is yours is a thing of wonder and joy. Never could I have expected so much."

Kennon looked down at her smudged face, streaked with the sudden rivulets of tears, and bitterness galled his throat. Dear God—let her be wrong, he prayed silently. Let it be pseudopregnancy this time. Let the tests be negative.

But they weren't. Unequivocally they confirmed Copper's diagnosis. Here was the proof he needed. The final test that would prove the Lani human. And he had no way of getting it where it would do any good. It would take at least four months of steady labor before the ship was ready, and he didn't have that sort of time. He was needed here and his prolonged absence would cause suspicion and investigation. Something would have to be done—but what? He couldn't take Copper off the island in an airboat. They were checked with microscopic care by Otpen One's IFF. A jeep didn't have enough range to take them to the mainland. And even if they got there they couldn't get off the planet. Alexander knew everything that happened on Kardon's two spaceports. The Egg was the only way, but the Egg was unfinished and unspaceworthy.

Frantically Kennon considered concealing Copper. He shook his head. It wouldn't work. It would be impossible to hide a baby on a place where every birth was recorded. Nor could one hide evidence of pregnancy in a Lani. Childbearing leaves telltale marks upon the body, and Copper, even if she could be concealed for the duration of her pregnancy, could never survive the sharp-eyed scrutiny of her fellows or the other humans. Questions would inevitably be asked.

There had to be a solution. He rubbed his forehead wearily. It was strange how so little a thing as the union of a spermatozoon and an ovum could produce so much trouble. He looked across the office at Copper placidly filing case cards. She wasn't worrying. With sublime faith, she was sure that he would find the answer, the one that would solve everything. He shuddered. The only logical solution was abortion—and that was unthinkable! He would not murder his child—nor would Copper permit it if he was capable of doing so.

It was almost a relief when his phone rang and Blalok's voice came cheerfully across the wire.

"Tried to get you about an hour ago," the superintendent said, "but your girl said you were busy."

"I was."

"You through now?"

"Yes."

"Well, get up to the fortress. Alexander just flew in and he's calling a meeting. Something important has come up."

Something important! A wave of ice rattled down Kennon's spine, and then he grinned feebly. Alexander didn't know. He couldn't know. It had to be something else.

"I'll be right up," he said, marveling at the calmness in his voice.

Kennon couldn't help comparing this meeting with the one a year ago. The location was different—the conference room in Alexandria was more formal than Blalok's parlor—but the same people were present: Alexander, Blalok, Jordan, and himself. Somehow Alexander seemed to have shrunk. He was no longer as impressive as he had been. But the man still radiated force, even though it didn't seem quite so overpowering. The year, Kennon thought, had done much to build his self-confidence. He felt assured rather than nervous.

"Good to see you, Kennon," Alexander said. "Reports say you're doing a good job."

"I can't claim the credit," Kennon said. "Eighty-five per cent of our success is due to co-operation from the operating staff. And that's Blalok's doing—he knocked the heads of the division managers together and they took care of their staffs. Otherwise we could have had a bad time."

"But you didn't," Alexander said. "And you were the motive force."

"I've darn near motivated myself out of a job," Kennon said. "They co-operate all too well nowadays."

"Which goes to prove that my theories on preventive medicine are right," Alexander said, turning to Blalok.

"It looks that way," Blalok admitted, "but that could be because you picked a good man."

"He's good in more ways than one," Alexander said. "Or did he tell you he saved Douglas's life out on Otpen One?"

"He's never said a word."

Alexander smiled. "Another point in his favor. He knows how to keep his mouth shut."

"Not when he's telling someone what to do about disease," Jordon interjected.

"Or telling someone off when they haven't followed directions," Blalok added.

"Better and better. I was sure that he was the one we needed when we first met."

Kennon felt his ears turn flaming red.

"But that's not the reason I brought you here. This isn't a Jac Kennon admiration society. I called you because I want to expand the Lani breeding program."

"Why?" Jordan asked.

Blalok stiffened. "You know my feeling about that, sir. I've never liked the idea of selling them. If that's what's in your mind——"

Alexander shook his head. "Simmer down," he said, as he seated himself at the head of the table. "There's going to be no selling. The Lani are too valuable for that. We'll need them more than the money they'd bring on the market. You see—I've acquired a planet out on the periphery. A place called Phoebe. One of our ships found it, and I staked a discovery claim on the major land mass, and the crew made lesser claims that covered all the available land. Last month the Brotherhood allowed the claims. Last week the crewmen sold me their land. Phoebe's a lovely place—quite a bit like Flora—and the ecological tests show it's capable of supporting mammalian life. Just before I came here I sent three shiploads of exterminators to clean it up and make it ready for us. It should be ready in two years."

"What sort of an ecology are you exterminating?" Jordan asked.

"Not that it makes any difference," Alexander said, "but it's mainly reptilian. Nothing over Group I. We'll restock with Floran animals."

Jordan sighed. "Since that's the way it is, it doesn't make any difference," he said. "But it could have. The Lani are sensitive to things like that. If they thought that they were walking in over a pile of bodies they'd do badly. It'd be like Olympus all over again. And we couldn't keep them from knowing. We talk—and we forget, but they'd tell each other—and they'd remember."

"I know," Alexander said, "somehow they've never forgotten that Grandfather trapped the last of the Lani males on Olympus."

Jordan nodded. "They can't stand the place. That's why we had to abandon the station."

"Does this new world have a moon?" Kennon asked abruptly.

"Yes—in fact it has two."

"Habitable?"

"No—they're too small to hold air. But men could live there in domes—but why do you?—oh! I see! I hadn't considered that point." Alexander's hand darted to the phone beside him. "Get me Albertsville," he snapped. "Yes, my offices—I want Mr. Oliver in purchasing and contracting. Hello—Ward? Alexander here. Yes—everything's fine. I have a job for you—use your scrambler-pattern two." Alexander dialed the scrambler code on the second dial at the base of the phone, effectively preventing eavesdropping by beam tappers. "Yes," he went on. "It's Project Phoebe. Have you secured title to the moons? You haven't? Well—you'd better do it before some of our competitors get bright ideas. Sure they know about the project—do you think they're stupid? Warren over at Consolidated practically told me that he was onto our scheme. So get title to those moons. Since they're uninhabitable and within the planet's primary field they come under the Spatial Debris Act and you should be able to get Kardonian title without any great amount of trouble. Naturally we want them.—For defense—what else? We'll have most of our eggs in that basket. No—I don't know how we overlooked that point. But if it wasn't for a bright young man out here we'd have left ourselves wide open. Now get cracking—get that leak plugged!" Alexander dropped the phone back in its cradle and sighed. "Well—that's buttoned up," he said. "Thanks, Kennon."

Kennon looked at Alexander's grinning face, his own impassive, but a shattering certainty exploded in his mind—*Alexander was a telepath!* That was his difference! That was the thing that made him feared and respected by his business associates. It wouldn't have been enough on the Central Worlds, where men knew of sensitives and took precautions against them. But out here on the periphery it was a deadly advantage.

"So I gave it away," Alexander said. "I suppose I was careless, but your thoughts about the moons shocked me."

"You practically told me once before, when you hired me," Kennon said, "but I never realized it."

"You were too excited then."

"I wouldn't know," Kennon said. "At any rate I didn't add the facts correctly." From somewhere deep in his memory an old quip came floating to the surface: "An executive is a man who picks brains—others' brains"! By that definition Alexander was an executive of the first class.

Alexander chuckled.

Suddenly Kennon wanted to run. Panic flooded him! What had he been thinking about? Had he thought of—two times two are four, four times four are sixteen, sixteen times sixteen are—let's see, six times sixteen is ninety-six, one times sixteen is—six, five, carry one—two—two hundred fifty-six. Two hundred fifty-six times——

"What's eating you?" Alexander demanded.

"I'm angry," Kennon said. "I told you the conditions I'd sign that contract, and you wrote a Peeper Clause into it. And then you peep in the worst way possible. There's no defense against a Telep unless you know about him; you've had my whole mind bare! You've violated my personal privacy like no man has done before. Sure I'm mad. I expected honesty from you—and you peep!" The anger was stronger now—a wave of raw emotion based on a lifetime of training in mutual respect of a man's privacy—a feeling intensified by his childhood environment of a crowded planetary ecology and the cramped crew quarters on a spaceship. To Kennon, Alexander had committed the ultimate sin.

"I can see I made a mistake by not telling you," Alexander said. His voice was cold. "But you have no right to insult me."

"I'm not saying it, am I?" Kennon snapped. The moonflower on the bookcase behind Alexander was a thing of beauty. Alexander liked beauty. He had said so, and the Great Hall below them bore it out. It was a lovely room. Those four bronze Lani in the fountain were works of art.

One of them looked remarkably like Copper. Copper in bronze. The little witch had probably posed for the casting. Maybe it had even been made from her body.

"They're all of Susy," Alexander said. "I can see why you are angry, and I don't blame you. But remember I warned you about Lani."

Copper—Kennon wrenched his thoughts back to the moonflower. It had twelve petals, limpid white on the borders shading to deep blue in the center from which the creamcolored stamen surrounded by transparent pistils sprang to burst into a golden glory of pollen that dripped in tiny yellow flecks to the broad petals below. It was a magnificent flower. There was nothing like it on Beta. That was a marvelous thing about flowers—wherever one went in the universe, plants used the same methods to fertilize their seed and spread their germ plasm. It was too bad that—Kennon jerked his attention to Alexander's face. He detested the thought that his mind was common property. A man should have something he can call his own. There had been a clinics instructor in Year Six who was a sensitive. The classes had protected themselves against his prying with a circlet—a thought screen—he had done it too. Maybe he had brought the circlet with him. If he did, no one was going to catch him without it. It was a dirty business, this reading of others' thought. Now where had he put that circlet? Was it among his old books—or was it with his instruments?

"Why don't you go back to your house and find it?" Alexander snapped. "As you are, you're nothing but a disruption. I want you in on this meeting, but not the way you're acting."

"I'm not going to act any other way until I get some protection from peeping," Kennon said grimly. "And if you think this is bad wait till I start going through comparative anatomy."

"What's the matter with you two?" Blalok asked.

"Be quiet," Alexander snapped. "This isn't your problem. Kennon is behaving like a spoiled child!"

"He's a telepath!" Kennon said. "And he didn't tell me."

"So what? I've known that for years."

"And you stand for it?"

"I'm a Mystic, not a Betan," Blalok said. "I don't have your insane desire for privacy."

"Go find that thought screen if you still have it!" Alexander said. "I don't want any more of this. You're making me ill!"

Kennon grinned thinly as he rose to his feet. It was a good thing he remembered Alexander was squeamish and didn't like anatomy. The door was to his left, an iris door with eight leaves—terribly old-fashioned. About ten steps away. Count them—one—two—three—

Alexander sighed as Kennon left the room. "I certainly pushed the panic button on that young man," he said. "He has a pathological attitude toward telepathy. Wonder what he has to hide that he wants privacy so badly? Even for a Betan this reaction was violent."

"Oh, I don't know. He's a pretty emotional sort. Maybe he hates to look like a fool. He's gotten himself mixed up with one of the Lani. Cute little thing by the name of Copper," Blalok said.

"Oh—that's it. I thought that was what he was hiding. A picture of a girl kept popping up." Alexander chuckled. "I suppose that's the trouble. A man hardly likes to look a fool, particularly to someone who has warned him. At that, I don't blame him. They are beautiful and affectionate. And even with their superstitions and tabus they're better than most humans."

"For pets," Blalok said heavily.

"They're not better at anything," Jordan demurred. "They can't be—man is the best and always will be."

"The eternal racial chauvinist," Alexander murmured. He turned his attention to Blalok. "But for awhile, Evald, I'd suggest you keep an eye on our young man. I still don't like his reaction. It was too violent—too defensive. I don't feel right about it. Perhaps Betans are more sensitive than most people but it seems to me that he's trying to conceal something. There was an undertone of fear—and something else —beneath his defenses."

"Couldn't you get any more than that?" Blalok asked. "You're pretty good at this mind-reading business."

"His defenses were remarkably good," Alexander said dryly.

Well—he'd done it now, Kennon thought. He found the thought-screen circlet sandwiched between two books on comparative neuroanatomy which he hadn't bothered to unpack. He slipped it on and connected the lead wires to a portable battery pack. There was a half-forgotten tingling as the weak field heterodyned his thought waves. Kennon sighed. If Alexander wasn't suspicious of him now the man was a fool. He'd done as well as he could with confusion and outrage, but it was hardly possible to hide behind superficialities. Even the most disciplined mind couldn't do that without some preparation. Undoubtedly his concern about

Copper had leaked through. He could only hope that other and more important things had not.

Well—he could go back to the conference now, but he would have to be doubly careful from now on. He couldn't make daily trips to Olympus. His reaction had killed that plan. Alexander would be suspicious now—and unusual actions would crystallize suspicion to certainty. Now he needed a reason to be in that area. And then he grinned. He had a reason—a good one—one that would fit in with Alexander's plans and his own. The only problem would be to make Alexander buy it—and that might be difficult. He'd have to work carefully—but with normal luck he could put the idea across. He crossed his fingers as he trudged back up the path to Alexandria.

The conference dragged on. Unlike most meetings, this one accomplished things—which was a tribute to Alexander's ability to keep the subject in hand. Details of the expansion program presented by Alexander were rapidly reduced to workable plans. They involved some rearrangement of existing facilities, and the construction of others. But the obvious snags were rapidly disposed of, and the whole revamped operation was outlined on paper in surprisingly few hours. A deadline date was set, construction was authorized, and in the morning the first steps in the practical implementation of the new program would be taken.

"Well, that's that," Alexander said with a sigh. "I think this calls for a drink."

"There's one more thing," Kennon said. "I know it isn't much, but Jordan's remark started me thinking."

"What remark?" Jordan asked.

"The one you made at the beginning about Phoebe possibly being like the Olympus Station. I've often wondered *why* that particular location has been so difficult to operate. Sure, I know the accepted explanation, but I think we should learn why it works and how to break a tabu. If we don't, we might be in for trouble."

"That's a good thought," Alexander said. "I tried to find out once, but all I could discover was that it was tabu. The Lani simply didn't like it. And despite the fact that I can read minds, I didn't learn any more than that. There's a certain sex-linkage to telepathy, as you probably know."

Kennon nodded.

"All I could discover was that their dislike of Olympus was a basic emotion rather than reasoned thought. They were nervous, irritable, disobedient, and un-co-operative while they were there—and even they didn't know why. It was merely tabu. We even tried youngsters—but the attitude was the same. I'd like to know more about that basic emotion."

"We should understand it," Kennon agreed. "If we transship a large number of Lani to a strange world, we should know their deepest motivations. We cannot take the chance that the transplant won't take, with all the money you're sinking into this project."

"You have a point there. Have you any suggestions about how to accomplish this?" Alexander's voice was interested.

"I have. Hire a psychologist. And reopen Olympus."

"It'll be the same story," Jordan said.

"Not if you apply experimental procedure," Kennon said. "Divide the place into a number of separate units in which groups of—say ten—Lani of various ages are kept. Let every group know where they are, but don't let them come in contact with one another. Observe them constantly. Put spy cells in the units. Couple them to recorders. Prepare a set of test situations and observe how each group performs. Question individuals under narcosynthesis. Observe and record any changes in physical condition—give them the works. Maybe we can collect some basic data that will indicate the answer."

"Not a bad idea," Alexander said.

"I don't like it," Jordan said. "It sounds cumbersome."

"It is," Kennon agreed. "But it may save a great deal of trouble later."

"I think you're right, Kennon," Blalok said. "We should know everything we can."

"What would you do first if you were heading this program?" Alexander asked. He eyed Kennon critically.

"Nothing," Kennon said promptly. "I'm not qualified to run an investigation like this. You need a specialist. I am a practitioner."

"Hmm—but you know experimental procedure."

"Naturally—but I do not have the training to prepare a program or evaluate its results. The only thing I could do would be to check the physical condition of the experimental groups."

"Could you set up the physical facilities?" Alexander asked.

"Possibly—I'd need a set of plans of the station, and I couldn't guarantee that the specialist wouldn't want to make changes. But the physical arrangements should be simple enough to construct."

"How long would it take you to prepare a plan?"

"I could have it by tomorrow, or perhaps a day later."

"If you can do it by then I'll stay over. I'd like to examine this proposal more closely. It has merit. That's the second constructive suggestion you've made tonight. Despite your peculiar desire for privacy, I'm glad you came back." Alexander smiled.

Kennon smiled back. Apparently the entrepreneur had taken the bait. But it was too early to tell whether he had swallowed it without reservation. It all depended upon how much had been given away before he had discovered that Alexander was a telepath. Perhaps Alexander was merely leading him on. There were too many intangibles, and there was no way of predicting how it would turn out. But he felt mildly optimistic.

Alexander closed the meeting, and Kennon left promptly. He had a good excuse. There was plenty of work to do if he was going to prepare an adequate plan for utilizing Olympus Station. Jordan went with him, but Blalok stayed behind. It was natural enough. Blalok was the administrator, but Kennon felt uneasy. Nor would he have felt any better if he could have heard what went on after he left.

Alexander looked quizzically at Blalok after the door closed behind the two men.

"Well, Evald, what do you think? Does it strike you that Kennon's sincere—or does it sound as though he has something up his sleeve?"

"If he does," Blalok said, "I don't know what it could be. I wouldn't take a job on Olympus if you gave it to me."

"If he doesn't know about the place," Alexander said thoughtfully, "it's probable that his suggestion was honest. I think it is but I'm not sure. He worries me now that I can't read him. I think I'll send Douglas back here to watch him."

"Why? In my book that'd be a poor choice. After all, you said Kennon saved his life. He should be grateful."

"You don't know Douglas," Alexander said. "He hates Kennon's guts for what he did."

"What did he do?"

"He made Douglas feel inferior. And there's no surer way to gain my cousin's undying enmity." Alexander laughed. "I know," he said. "He'd like to kill me, too."

Blalok shrugged.

"But in the meantime I want you to keep an eye on Kennon. If his outline is all right, I'm going to authorize him to set up this experiment. I want to give him every possible chance. I like him—and he's done good work. I wouldn't want him to feel that I distrust him."

"Which you do, of course," Blalok said dryly.

Alexander smiled. "Actually," he said with equal dryness, "I distrust everyone."

CHAPTER XVI

"If you think this job is easy, you have another think coming," Kennon said bitterly. "I hired out as a veterinarian, not as a nursemaid for a bunch of psychoneurotic humans and superstitious Lani. The place is jinxed, they tell me.—Ha! Jinxed! Sure it's jinxed! What job wouldn't be with a bunch of goofballs like those I've got working on it.

"I can't keep a Lani here for two weeks without having her throw a catfit, and the superstitious idiots are affecting the men—who ought to know better! I wish I'd never have opened my big mouth to Alexander! As far as I'm concerned he can take this job and——"

"Hey—take it easy, man!" Blalok said. "You're heading straight for a nervous breakdown."

"And why shouldn't I?" Kennon asked. "Nothing goes right. There's always trouble. I order materials—they don't arrive. There's worker trouble, equipment trouble, installation trouble. Everybody's cutting corners, trying to get done faster and away sooner—and all they do is mess up work that should have been done right the first time. We should have been finished last week, but we have another week to go, at least unless some bumble-fingered beanbrain gets another bright idea that sets us back again. I'm sick to death of it!"

"I know, I know," Blalok said soothingly, "and I'm sorry."

"Sorry? What good is that? You and Jordan come up here in relays. Just what do you think you'll find? Or has Alexander dragged you into keeping an eye on me because I don't like someone snooping inside my skull?"

"It's not that," Blalok said. "It's just——"

"Oh, don't make excuses. You know and I know the Bossman is suspicious." Kennon shrugged. "Normally I wouldn't blame him but it's a damned nuisance with things the way they are. All we have is one more bay and a hall to finish— but if——"

"Now wait a minute," Blalok said. "Get the kink out of your neck and simmer down. Sure—the Boss-man told us to keep an eye on you—but that's not why I'm here this time."

"Well?"

"Douglas came back this morning."

"What for?"

"I don't know." Blalok's face wore the noncommittal look it always wore when he was taking liberties with the truth.

"You're probably the worst liar in the galaxy," Kennon chuckled. "He's here to breathe down my neck, isn't he?"

Blalok nodded.

"Keep him off my back for another week and he can breathe all he wants to. I'll be done then."

"I can't promise a thing."

Kennon shrugged. "It's too much to ask, I guess."

"But I can try," Blalok added.

"That's enough for me." Kennon grinned. "Has he turned Alexandria into a shambles yet?"

"Not yet, but everyone's uneasy."

"I can't blame them. That young fellow's undiluted poison. By the way, how does he look?"

"About the same."

"The medics must have done a good job," Kennon said.

"The Boss-man shipped him to Beta for treatment," Blalok said. "He didn't trust the docs out here."

"That figures. At any rate Douglas couldn't have gone to a better place."

"What happened to him?"

"He stuck his nose where he shouldn't," Kennon said pointedly.

Blalok stiffened.

"I'm sorry, Evald. Even if you knew, I couldn't talk about it. What I know about Douglas is classified!"

"Well—Douglas is doing plenty of talking. Claims his stay in the hospital was all your fault."

Kennon shrugged. "That's his opinion. And as long as he stays out of my way he's welcome to it."

Blalok looked at Kennon's haggard face with mild concern. "Doc," he said, "you'd better take it easy. You're going to pieces."

"I'll be through here in another week. I'll have this all wrapped up."

"Providing you're not wrapped up first."

"Eh?"

"In a shroud. You look like a walking corpse."

Kennon chuckled wearily. "Sometimes I feel like one. But I'd like to get this job finished."

"Well, I'll do what I can," Blalok said. "I'll try to keep him down at Alexandria for a few days."

"It'll be enough," Kennon said. More than enough—he added mentally. The coils of fuel wire were ready to load, and the power slugs for the ship's reactor were already stored in the power plant building here at Olympus. Three more days and the old spacer would be as ready to fly as she would ever be. And after that, it was in the lap of fate.

He ushered Blalok to his jeep and watched until he disappeared.

"I'm getting to be a first-class liar," he remarked wryly to himself as he turned back to the temporary quarters he was occupying at the station. "And the bad thing about it is that I'm actually enjoying it."

A few weeks ago an admission like that would have been inconceivable. It was odd, he thought, how one thing led to another and produced an end that could not be foreseen. Now he could lie and dissemble with the best. He had no compunction about falsifying a requisition, or stealing what he could not obtain with apparent honesty. His character had sunk to an all-time low, he reflected with grim humor as he walked into the shadow of the main building. Neither Blalok's nor Jordan's frequent visits bothered him. Both men were creatures of habit and both were married. They stayed home at night—and it was nighttime that he worked on the spacer. The project afforded him a perfect cover and it was only minutes by jeep away from the crater.

Even so, the double duty was an appalling task. And it would have been impossible if it wasn't for Copper. Her quick fingers, keen eyesight, and uncanny memory made the work seem simple, and neither the tediousness of repairing miles of circuitry nor the depressing environment of Olympus Station seemed to bother her. While he worked with the men on the project she restored and reassembled circuits in his quarters and at night they replaced them in the old ship. And the God-Egg was rapidly becoming operational.

Kennon wondered what it was about Copper that made her so different from the rest. Olympus didn't bother her at all. In fact she seemed to thrive on the depressing atmosphere that filled the Station. Perhaps it was because she had violated the tabu about the God-Egg so often that ordinary superstition had no effect upon her. He shrugged. He had troubles enough without worrying about Copper's motivations, and not the least of these was taking the God-Egg into space.

Kennon looked forward to blast-off with distinct misgivings. There was too much about the ancient spacer that was strange—and too much that was terrifying.

Basically the ship was an ion-jet job with atomic primaries and a spindizzy converter that might possibly take her up as high as middle yellow Cth—far enough to give her a good turn of speed, but not enough to compensate for timelag. Her screens were monstrosities, double polyphase lattices that looked about as spacetight as so many sieves. There were no acceleration dampers, no temporal compensators, no autopilot, no four-space computer, and the primaries operated on nuclear rather than binding energy. The control chairs weren't equipped with forcefields, but instead had incredibly primitive safety webs that held one in place by sheer tensile strength. Taking a ship like that into space was an open invitation to suicide. A man needed a combination of foolhardy bravery and incredible fatalism to blast off in a can like this. He had the stimulus, but the knowledge of what he would face troubled him more than he cared to admit. More and more, as he understood the ship, he was amazed at the courage of the ancients who had blithely leaped into hyperspace in these flying coffins with no more motivation than to see what was beyond the nearest star. And in ships more primitive than this men had swept through the star systems nearest Earth in the outward expansion of the First Millennium.

He sighed. The breed of man must have been tough in the old days—and he'd soon be finding out if any of that ancient toughness remained.

He opened the door to his quarters.

Copper was sitting in his favorite chair, a pile of completed assemblies neatly stacked beside her, and a disorderly file of crumpled cloth at her feet. Her face was sullen as she looked up at him. "I've had about all of this I'm going to take," she said mutinously as she stirred the heap of cloth with a bare foot. "Not even you are going to make me wear those—*things!*"

Kennon sighed. It was the same old story. For months he had been trying patiently to indoctrinate Copper with a minimum of civilized habits, but she was quite literally a savage. In her entire lifetime she had never worn clothing, and to encase her body in hose, kilts, blouse, and sandals was a form of torture. She scratched, wiggled, and twisted at the garments until she looked as bad as she felt, and would usually finish a session by tearing off the offending clothes and sulking. She was doing it now.

"You must act like a civilized human being," Kennon said mildly. "You're simply going to have to learn to wear these clothes properly."

"Why? I'm more comfortable as I am."

"That's not the point. You are going to be living in human society and you must act human. The only planet where you could get away with nudity is Santos, and we're not going there."

"Why not?"

"I've explained it time and again. We'll have to go to Beta. That's the only place I know where you'll have a fair hearing. And on Beta people wear clothes. They have to. It's cold, even in summer, and in the wintertime, there's snow."

"What's snow?"

"Ice crystals that fall like rain, but I've told you this before."

"And I still don't believe it."

"Believe it or not you're going to wear those things. Now put them on!"

She looked at him with mutiny on her face. "All right, slave driver," she muttered as she picked up the clothing, "but I hope you'll itch someday and be unable to scratch."

"And try to wear those garments more gracefully. You make them look like a sack."

"They feel like one. I keep thinking that all I need is a tag around my neck."

"You haven't much time to get used to them," Kennon said. "We're leaving this week."

"So soon?"

"Yes—and you'll wear those things to the ship, into the ship, and all the time we're on the ship. You'll keep wearing clothing until it looks right."

"Slave driver!" Copper hissed.

"Slave," Kennon answered equably.

Copper giggled. The sound was utterly unexpected, and completely incongruous. That was the wonder of her, Kennon reflected. Her mercurial temperament made life something that was continually exciting. She was a never-ending delight.

CHAPTER XVII

It was the last trip. Kennon loaded the jeep with the last-minute items he would need. The four reactor cores in their lead cases went aboard last and were packed inside a pile of lead-block shielding.

He helped Copper in and looked back without regret as the bulk of Olympus Station vanished below him in the dusk. The last of the work crew had left that afternoon. The station was ready for occupancy. His assignment had been completed. He felt an odd pleasure at having finished the job. Alexander might not be happy about his subsequent actions, but he could have no complaint about what he did while he was here.

"Well—say good-bye to Flora," he said to Copper.

"I don't want to," she said. "I don't want to leave."

"You can't stay. You know that."

She nodded. "But that doesn't make me any less regretful."

"Regretful?"

"All right—scared. We're going to try to make the God-Egg fly again. Not only is it sacrilege, but as you've often said, it's dangerous. I have no desire to die."

"You have two courses——"

"I know—you've pointed them out often enough," Copper said. "And since you decided to go I'd go with you even though I knew the Egg would blow up."

"You're quite a girl," Kennon said admiringly. "Did I ever tell you that I love you?"

"Not nearly often enough," Copper said. "You could do it every day and I'd never get tired of hearing it."

The jeep settled over the lava wall. "We'll leave it in the passageway when we're through," Kennon said. "Maybe it will survive blast-off."

"Why worry about it?" Copper asked.

"I hate destroying anything needlessly," Kennon said. "And since we have plenty of time, we might as well be neat about our departure."

He was wrong, of course, but he didn't know that.

Douglas Alexander checked the radarscope and whistled in surprise at the picture it revealed. "So that's where he's going," he said softly to himself. "Cousin Alex was right as usual." He grimaced unpleasantly. "He's up to something—that's for sure." His face twisted into an expression that was half sneer, half triumph. "This is going to be fun." He moved the controls, and his airboat, hovering silently at five thousand meters, dropped toward the ground in free fall as Douglas loosened the Burkholtz in the holster at his waist. "But what is he doing?" he muttered. The question hung unanswered in the still air of the cabin as the airboat dropped downward.

Douglas hadn't been impressed with Blalok's attempt at a delaying action. Normally he might have been, but his fear of his cousin was greater than his respect for Blalok. The superintendent had only succeeded in accomplishing something he had not intended when he had tried to dissuade Douglas from visiting Kennon. He had made Douglas cautious. The airboat and long-range surveillance had been the result. For the past two nights Douglas had hung over Olympus Station, checking the place—to leave at dawn when the new day's work began. For two nights Kennon had been lucky. He had departed for the Egg shortly before Douglas took up his station, and had returned after the watcher had called it a night and had returned home. But this last night, Kennon left late—and his departure was noted.

"Wonder who's the girl with him?" Douglas said as the boat plunged down. "Well, I'll be finding out in a minute."

Kennon's head jerked upward at the sound of air whistling past the airboat's hull, and a wave of icy coldness swept through his chest. There was no question that he was discovered. His shoulders sagged.

"Well—it was a good try," he said bitterly as Copper looked at him with sudden terror on her face.

"I don't *want* to die," she wailed.

"You won't—not if I can help it," Kennon said. "Move away from me—quickly!"

"But——"

"Do as I say!" Kennon's voice was sharp. "And keep that hood over your face."

The airboat settled softly on the ash in front of him, the door snapped open and Douglas dropped to the ground, Burkholtz jutting from his pudgy fist.

"My, my," Douglas said, "what have we here? Dr. Kennon and a woman! I thought better of you than that, Doctor. And

119

all dressed up in antiradiation suits. This *is* interesting. Just what are you doing up here on the mountain so late at night —prospecting?"

"You might call it that," Kennon said. His body sagged with relief. Douglas—thank Ochsner it was Douglas! He was running true to form—talking when he should have been shooting.

Douglas jerked his head toward Copper, standing a few feet to his left. "Who is she?"

"None of your business," Kennon snapped, hoping that his outburst covered Copper's gasp of surprise and fear, and knowing that it didn't.

"I'm making it my business. There's something funny going on around here."

Kennon blinked. Could it be that Douglas didn't *know*? Had he been watching them on *radar*? Durilium was radar-transparent. It absorbed and dissipated electromagnetic waves rather than reflecting them. For a second he felt a tiny surge of hope.

"Stand where you are," Douglas said as he stepped over to the half-paralyzed Copper and jerked the hood back from her face. For a moment he looked puzzled. "Just who are you?" he demanded. "I don't recall seeing you before." And then recognition dawned. "Old Doc's Lani!" he gasped.

"She works for me now," Kennon said.

Douglas laughed. It wasn't a nice sound. "All dressed up?" he asked. "Nice work."

"That's my fault," Kennon said.

"You know the rules," Douglas said. "I could blast you both."

"Go ahead," Kennon said, "but if you do, you'll never find out what we're doing up here."

Douglas hesitated. Kennon's voice was flat and filled with utter conviction.

"There's a reason why Copper's wearing that suit," Kennon continued, "and you won't know that either."

The Burkholtz swiveled around to point at Kennon's belly. "I've had about enough of this. Let's have it. Tell me what you're doing here!"

"I'll do better than that," Kennon said promptly. "I'll show you. You'll be surprised at what we've uncovered." He made his muscles relax, and forced himself to speak naturally. Copper, he noted, was still rigid with terror. The Alexanders —any of them—were everything he had said they were. They were the masters here. And despite Copper's boast, she was as susceptible to their influence as any other Lani.

"All right," Douglas said, "show me this thing I'd never be able to find without your help." He half turned to Copper. "Stay where you are, Lani," he said. "Don't move until I come back."

"Yes, Man Douglas," Copper replied. Her voice was flat, colorless, and submissive.

Kennon shuddered. He had never heard precisely that tone from her before. One word from Douglas and she had become a zombie—a mindless muscle preparation that existed only to obey. Anger filled him—anger that one he loved could be ordered by someone who wasn't worth a third of her—anger that she obeyed—anger at his own impotence and frustration. It wasn't a clean anger. It was a dark, red-splashed thing that struggled and writhed inside him, a fierce unreasoning rage that seethed and bubbled yet could not break free. For an instant, with blinding clarity, Kennon understood the feelings of the caged male Lani on Otpen One. And he sympathized.

"Follow me," he said and started around the ship.

"Stay—no—go ahead," Douglas said, "but remember, I'm right behind you."

Kennon walked straight up to the pit and pointed down at the dark bulk of the Egg, concealed in the shadows of the bottom.

"That's it," he said.

"What? I don't see anything," Douglas said suspiciously.

"Here—I'll shine a light." Kennon reached for his belt.

"No you don't! I know that trick. You're not going to blind me. Take that torch loose carefully—that's it—now hand it to me." Douglas' hand closed over the smooth plastic. Cautiously he turned on the beam and directed it downward.

"A spacer!" he gasped. "How did that get here?" He leaned forward to look into the pit as a dark shadow materialized behind him.

Kennon choked back the involuntary cry of warning that rose in his throat. Copper! His muscles tensed as her arm came up and down—a shadow almost invisible in the starlight. The leaning figure of Douglas collapsed like a puppet whose strings had been suddenly released. The torch dropped from his hand and went bouncing and winking down the wall of the pit, followed by Douglas—a limp bundle of arms and legs that rotated grotesquely as he disappeared down the slope. Starlight gleamed on the Burkholtz lying on the lip of the crater, where it had fallen from his hand.

"I told you that not even Man Alexander could order me

121

since I gave my love to you," Copper said smugly as she peered over the edge of the pit, a chunk of lava gripped in one small capable hand. "Maybe this proves it."

"Douglas isn't Alexander," Kennon said slowly as he picked up the blaster, "but I believe you."

"Didn't I act convincingly?" she said brightly.

"Very," he said. "You fooled me completely."

"The important thing was that I fooled Douglas."

"You did that all right. Now let's get him out of that pit."

"Why?"

"The jet blast will fry him when we take off."

"What difference would that make?"

"I told you," Kennon said, "that I never destroy things unnecessarily—not even things like Douglas."

"But he would have destroyed you."

"That's no excuse for murder. Now go back to the jeep and fetch a rope. I'll go down and get him out."

"Do we have to bother with him?" Copper asked, and then shrugged. It was an eloquent gesture expressing disgust, resignation, and unwilling compliance in one lift of smoothly muscled shoulders.

"There's no question about it," Kennon said. "You're becoming more human every day."

He chuckled as he slid over the edge of the pit following the path Douglas had taken a moment before. He found him sitting on a pile of ashes, shaking his head.

"What happened?" Douglas asked querulously. There was fear in his voice.

"Copper hit you on the head with a rock," Kennon said as he bent over and retrieved the torch, still burning near Douglas' feet.

"The Lani?" Douglas' voice was incredulous.

"Not a Lani," Kennon corrected. "She's as human as you or I."

"That's a lie," Douglas said.

"Maybe this spacer's a lie too. Her ancestors came in it— a pair of humans named Alfred and Melissa Weygand. They were Christian missionaries from a planet called Heaven out in Ophiuchus Sector. Went out to convert aliens and landed here when their fuel ran out." Kennon paused. "That was about four millennia ago. Their descendants, naturally, reverted to barbarism in a few generations, but there's enough evidence in the ship to prove that the Lani were their children."

"But the tails—the differences—the failure of the test," Douglas said.

"Mutation," Kennon replied. "Those old spindizzy converters weren't too choosy about how they scattered radiation. And they had come a long way." He paused, looking down at Douglas, feeling a twinge of pity for the man. His world was crumbling. "And there was no other human blood available to filter out their peculiarities. It might have been done during the first couple of generations, but constant inbreeding fixed the genetic pattern."

"How did you discover this?" Douglas asked.

"Accident," Kennon said briefly.

"You'll never be able to prove they're human!" Douglas said.

"The ship's log will do that."

"Not without a humanity test—they can't pass that."

"Sorry to disappoint you. Your grandfather used the wrong sort of sperm. Now if there had been a Betan in the crew——"

"You mean she's *pregnant!*"

Kennon nodded. "There's been mutation on Beta," he said. "And it's apparently a similar one to hers. Betan-Lani matings are fertile."

Douglas's shoulders sagged, and then straightened. "I don't believe it," he said. "You're just a damned sneaking spy. Somehow or other you got a spacer in here after you wormed your way into Cousin Alex's confidence—and now you're going to space out with the nucleus of a new farm. Just wait. When Alex learns of this the galaxy'll be too small to hold you."

"Don't babble like a fool!" Kennon said with disgust. "How could I land a spacer here without being spotted? You sound like a two-credit novel. And even if I did—would it be a can like this?" Kennon played the torch over the blue-black durilium protruding from the ashes.

Douglas' eyes widened as he took in the details of construction. "What an antique!" he blurted. "Where did you get this can?"

"I found it here."

"Tell me another one."

"You won't believe," Kennon said flatly, "because you don't dare believe. You have a mental block. You've killed, maimed, tortured—treated them like animals—and now your mind shrinks from admitting they're human. You know what will happen if the old court decision is reversed. It will wreck your little empire, dry up your money, break you—and you can't stand the thought of that. You don't dare let us leave, yet you can't stop us because I have your blaster and I'd just as soon shoot you as look at your rotten face. Now get on your feet and start climbing if you want to stay alive. We're getting out of here, and you'll fry inside this pit."

"Where are you taking me?"

"Back to your airboat. I'm going to tie you up and set you off on autopilot. You'll be able to get loose quickly enough but it'll be too late to stop us. We'll be gone, and you can think of how you'll manage to face the human race."

"I hope you blow yourself and that antique clear out of space."

"We might. But you'll never know for sure. But mark this —if I live I'll be back with the Brotherhood. You can count on it."

They struggled up the side of the pit and halted, panting, on the rim. "How much radiation was down there?" Douglas asked worriedly.

"Not enough to hurt you."

"That's good." Douglas accepted the statement at face value, a fact which failed to surprise Kennon. "You know," he said, "I've been around Lani all my life. And I know that they're not human. No self-respecting human would take a tenth of what they put up with."

"Their ancestors didn't," Kennon said. "They fought to the end. But your Grandfather was a smart man even though he was a Degrader."

"He *wasn't!*" Douglas exploded. "No Alexander is a Degrader."

"He realized," Kennon went on, "that he'd never succeed in enslaving the Lani unless he separated the sexes. And since women are more subjective in their outlook—and more pliable—he picked them for his slaves. The males he retired to stud. Probably the fact that there were more women than men helped him make up his mind.

"In every society," Kennon went on inexorably, "there are potential freeman and potential slaves. The latter invariably outnumber the former. They're cowards: the timid, the unsacrificing—the ones that want peace at any price—the ones who will trade freedom for security. Those were the ones who hid rather than risk their lives fighting the aggressor. Those were the ones who survived. Old Alexander had a ready-made slave cadre when he finished off the last of the warriors. For four centuries the survivors have been bred and selected to perpetuate slave traits. And the system works. The men don't want freedom—they want liberty to kill each other. The women don't want freedom—they want males. And they'd serve them precisely as the Sarkian women serve their menfolk. You've killed any chance they had to become a civilization. It's going to take generations perhaps before they're reoriented. There's plenty you Alexanders should answer for."

"If there's any fault, it's yours," Douglas snarled. "We were doing all right until you came here. We'd still be doing all right if I had shot you both." His shoulders sagged. "I should have killed you when I had the chance," he said bitterly.

"But you didn't," Kennon said, "and to show my gratitude I'm letting you get away with a whole skin. I don't expect you to be grateful, but at least you'll not be on my conscience. I don't enjoy killing, not even things like you."

Douglas sneered. "You're soft—a soft sentimental fool."

"Admitted," Kennon said, "but that's my nature."

"Yet you'd destroy the family, wreck Outworld Enterprises, and throw a whole world into chaos over a few thousand animals. I don't understand you."

"They're human," Kennon said flatly.

"Admitting they might once have been, they're not now."

"And whose fault is that?"

"Not ours," Douglas said promptly. "If there is any fault it's that of the court who decided they were humanoid."

"You didn't help any."

"Why should we? Does one treat a shrake like a brother? —or a varl?—or a dog? We treat them like the animals they are. And we've done no worse with the Lani. Our consciences are clear."

Kennon laughed humorlessly. "Yet this clear conscience makes you want to kill me, so you can keep on treating them as animals—even though you know they're human."

"I know nothing of the sort. But you're right about the killing. I'd kill you cheerfully if I had the chance. It's our necks if you get away with this. Of course, you probably won't, but why take the chance. I like my neck more than I like yours."

"You're honest at any rate," Kennon admitted. "And in a way I don't blame you. To you it's probably better to be a rich slaver living off the legacy of a Degrader than a penniless humanitarian. But you've lost your chance."

Douglas screamed with rage. He whirled on Kennon, his face a distorted mask of hate.

"Hold it!" Kennon barked. "I don't want to kill you, but I'll burn a hole clear through your rotten carcass if you make another move. I have no love for your kind."

Douglas spat contemptuously. "You haven't got the guts," he snarled. But he didn't move.

"Just stand still—very still," Kennon said softly. The iron in his voice was not hidden by the quiet tone.

Douglas shivered. "I'll get you yet," he said, but there was no force in the threat.

"Here's the rope you wanted," Copper said as she emerged abruptly from the darkness. "I had a hard time finding it."

"You haven't been too long," Kennon said. "Now tie Douglas' hands behind him while I keep him covered."

"It's a pleasure," Copper murmured.

CHAPTER XVIII

"I'm frightened," Copper said, twisting uncomfortably in the shock chair beside Kennon's.

"After you have been so brave?" Kennon asked. "That's nonsense. It's just nervous reaction. Now web in like I showed you. It's time for blast-off. We don't dare wait much longer."

"All right—but I have a feeling that this isn't right. Something is going to go wrong."

"I hope you don't have precognition." Kennon smiled. "I've checked everything. The ship is as good as she'll ever be. There's nothing more that we can do."

"There's one consolation," Copper said wanly. "At least we'll die together."

"There's a better chance that we'll live together."

"I hope so."

"Ready?" Kennon asked.

She nodded.

He flipped the switches that would send the fuel rods into the reactor. Below them a soft, barely audible whine ascended the sonic scale to a point of irritating inaudibility. Kennon smiled. The spindizzy was functioning properly. He flipped a second bank of switches and a dull roar came from the buried stern. Ashes and pumice heated to incandescence were blown through the air. Molten drops of radioactive lava skittered across the durilium hull as Kennon advanced the power. The whole stern of the ship was immersed in a seething lake of boiling rock as the Egg lifted slowly with ponderous dignity into the night sky.

"Hang on!" Kennon said. "I'm going to hyper." His hand moved a red lever and the Egg shimmered and vanished with a peculiar wrenching motion into an impossible direction that the mind could not grasp. And the interceptor missile from Otpen One nosed through the space the Egg had occupied.

"We made it!" Kennon said, looking across the writhing semifluid control board, shifting oddly in the harsh yellow monochromatic light that pervaded the cabin. The screens were leaking like sieves, but they were holding well enough to keep Cth yellow from being anything more than an annoyance. He glanced over at Copper, a fantastically elongated Copper who looked like a madman's dream of chaos.

And Copper screamed! The sound echoed and re-echoed, dying away with a lingering discordant reverberation that made his skin tingle.

"Copper! It's all right! It's all right! Stop it!"

Copper screamed again and her elongated figure suddenly foreshortened and collapsed into a small writhing ball from which two small pink hands emerged clutching at a gelid mass of air that flowed sluggishly around them.

And Kennon knew what he had forgotten! Hyperspace with leaky screens was nothing to inflict upon an unprepared mind. It is one thing to endure partial exposure after months of training, with experienced medics standing by to help you through the shock phase, but quite another to be thrust from a safe and sheltered existence into the mind shattering distortions of the Cth continuum.

The Egg was old. Her screens, never good at best, were hardly more than filters. Through the hull, through the drive lattice, the viciously distorted Cth environment seeped into the ship turning prosaic shapes of controls and instruments into writhing masses of obscene horror that sent extensions wiggling off into nothingness at eye-aching angles. A spaceman could take this—knowing it wasn't real—but a tyro could not.

Copper collapsed. Her mind, assaulted by sensations no untrained person should experience, went into shock. But she wasn't granted the mercy of unconsciousness. Terrified by a pseudo reality that surpassed her wildest nightmares, she stared wide-eyed at the control room and the thing that had been Kennon. She screamed until her throat was raw, until the monster beside her touched her with Kennon's hands. Then, mercifully, she felt a stinging in her arm and all sensation ceased.

Kennon stared glumly at the controls. Fleming alone knew how many objective years were passing outside as they hurtled through four-space. Subjectively it would only be hours aboard the Egg, but a decade—or maybe a century—might pass outside this mad universe where neither time nor speed had meaning. The old ships didn't have temporal compensators, nor could they travel through upper bands of Cth where subjective and objective time were more nearly equal. They were trapped in a semi-stasis of time as the ship fled on through the distorted monochromatic regions that bypassed normal space.

The Egg slipped smoothly out of the hyper jump, back into the normal universe. Beta floated above them, the blue shield of her atmosphere shining softly in the light of Beta's sun.

"Couldn't hit it that good again in a hundred tries," Kennon gloated. "Halfway across the galaxy—and right on the nose." He looked at the shock chair beside him. Copper was curled into a tight ball inside the confining safety web, knees drawn up, back bent, head down—arms wrapped protectingly around her legs—the fetal position of catatonic shock.

He shook her shoulder—no response. Her pulse was thready and irregular. Her breathing was shallow. Her lips were blue. Her condition was obvious—space shock—extreme grade. She'd need medical attention if she was going to live. And she'd need it fast!

"Just why, you educated nitwit," he snarled at himself, "didn't you have sense enough to give her that injection of Somnol *before* we hypered! You haven't the sense of a decerebrate Capellan grackle!"

He turned on the radio. "Emergency!" he said. "Any station! Space-shock case aboard. Extreme urgency."

"Identify yourself—give your license. Over."

"What port are you?"

"Hunterstown—will you please identify? Over."

"Your co-ordinates," Kennon snapped. "Over."

"280.45—67.29 plus. Repeat—request your identification."

"Pilot Kennon, Jac, Beta 47M 26429. I have no I.D. for the ship—and you'll see why when I land. Over."

"Hunterstown Port to Kennon. You are not—repeat *not*—cleared to land. Go into orbit and report your position. Over."

"Sorry, Hunterstown. You wouldn't have checked in if you didn't have room, and a hospital. This is an emergency. I'm setting down. Out."

"But——" The words got no farther. Kennon was already spinning the ship.

"All right—we have you on the scope. But this is a class

one violation. You may come in on Landing Beam One."

"Sorry. I have no GCA."

"What?—what sort of ship are you flying?" The voice was curious.

"I'm matching intrinsics over your port. Talk me in when I break through the overcast."

"Talk you in?"

"That's right. My instruments are obsolete."

"Great Halstead! What else?"

"I have an Ion drive. Plus two radioactive."

"Oh no!—And you still want to come in?"

"I have to. My passenger's in shock. She's going to have a baby."

"All right—I'll try to get you down in one piece."

"Have an ambulance ready," Kennon said.

Kennon lowered the Egg through the overcast. Ground control picked him up smoothly and took him down as though it had been rehearsed. The Egg touched down in the radioactive area of the port. Decontamination jets hissed, sluicing the ship to remove surface contamination.

"Ochsner! what sort of a ship *is* that?" Ground Control's startled voice came over the annunciator.

"It's an old one," Kennon said.

"That's a gross understatement. Stand by for boarders. Ambulance coming up."

Kennon opened the airlock and two radiation-suited men entered. "At least you had sense enough to wear protective clothing in this hotbox," one said as they carefully unwebbed Copper and carried her out of the lock. "You wait here. The Port Captain wants to see you."

"Where are you taking her? What Center?" Kennon asked.

"What should you care? You've nearly killed her. The idea of taking a pregnant woman up in this death trap! What in Fleming's name's the matter with your brain?"

"I had to," Kennon said. "I had to. It was a matter of life and death." For once, he thought wryly, the cliché was true.

The Betan's face behind the transparent helmet was disgusted and unbelieving. "I hear that sort of thing every day," he said. "Am I supposed to believe it?"

"You'd believe it if you'd have been where I was," Kennon muttered. "Now—where are you taking her?" he demanded.

The man arched blond eyebrows. "To the local Medical Center—where else? There's only one in this area."

"Thanks," Kennon said.

He watched the ambulance flit off as he waited for the

Spaceport Patrol. There was no further need for the protection suit, so he peeled it off and hung it in the control-room locker. Copper was right, he mused. It did itch.

The Port Captain's men were late as usual—moving gingerly through the radiation area. A noncom gestured for him to enter their carryall. "Port Captain wants to see you," he said.

"I know," Kennon replied.

"You should have waited upstairs."

"I couldn't. It was a matter of medicine," Kennon said.

The noncom's face sobered. "Why didn't you say so? All you said was that it was an emergency."

"I've been away. I forgot."

"You shouldn't have done that. You're a Betan, aren't you?"

Kennon nodded.

They drove to the Port Office, where Kennon expected—and got—a bad time from the port officials. He filled out numerous forms, signed affidavits, explained his unauthorized landing, showed his spaceman's ticket, defended his act of piloting without an up-to-date license, signed more forms, entered a claim for salvage rights to the Egg, and finally when the Legal Division, the Traffic Control Division, the Spaceport Safety Office, Customs, Immigration, and Travelers Aid had finished with him, he was ushered into the presence of the Port Captain.

The red-faced chunky officer eyed him with a cold stare. "You'll be lucky, young man, if you get out of this with a year in Correction. Your story doesn't hang together."

It didn't, Kennon thought. But there was no sense telling all of it to a Port Captain. Under no circumstances could the man be any help to him. He had neither the power nor the prestige to request a Brotherhood Board of Inquiry. In rank, he was hardly more than a glorified Traffic Control officer. It would do no good to tell him an improbable tale of slavery on a distant planet. The only thing to do was wait out the storm and hope it would pass. If worst came to worst he'd use his rank, but he'd made enough stir already. He doubted if the Captain had authority to order him into Detention—but he was certain to get a lecture. These minor officials loved to tell someone off. He gritted his teeth. He'd endure it for Copper's sake—and to get out of here quietly. Alexander would undoubtedly have agents posted by now, and his only chance for temporary freedom of action was to get out of here with as little fuss as possible.

He sat quietly, his flushed face and tight jaw muscles betraying his impatience as the Captain paced up and down and talked on and on. The man sounded like he could go for hours. With increasing impatience Kennon listened to the cadenced flow of complaint and condemnation, occasionally inserting a "Yes, sir" or "Sorry, sir" or "No, sir" as the words flowed around him.

However, there had to be a breaking point somewhere, and the monotony was beginning to wear his temper thin. Another five minutes, he reflected, was about all he could take.

The door chime rang softly.

"Come in," the Port Captain said, breaking off in mid-tirade. The change in his manner was so abrupt that Kennon couldn't help smiling.

A young blond man in an interne's gray uniform entered the room.

"Yes, Doctor," the Port Captain said. "What can I do for you?"

"Do you have a Jac Kennon here? Dr. Jac Kennon?"

"Did you say *doctor?*" the Port Captain said in a half-strangled voice.

"You never let me tell you," Kennon said mildly, "that my landing here was a matter of medicine. Technically you have contributed to a delay in treatment."

The Port Captain's face paled. "Why didn't you *say* something?" he said.

"Against your gale of wind I would be but a faint breeze," Kennon said coldly. He turned to the interne. "I'm Dr. Kennon." They bowed formally to each other.

"I'm Smalley, sir, from the medical center. Dr. Brainard sends his compliments and requests that you join him for consultation."

"The Port Captain—" Kennon began.

"Don't worry about it, Doctor. I'll relinquish responsibility to Dr. Brainard," the Captain said.

"I have placed a formal written request with your office," Smalley said stiffly. "You are relieved of further charge. Dr. Kennon is urgently needed. It is a matter of medicine."

The Captain looked relieved. On Beta it was poor policy to interfere with the doings of doctors and engineers—or even doctors of philosophy.

"Very well. He's yours—and I'm glad to be rid of him." The Port Captain bowed to Kennon and Smalley and stalked out of the office.

"Pompous little man," Kennon observed, "but he certainly can talk."

"Oh—you know these Administrative people," the interne

said depreciatingly. "One mustn't mind them. They're necessary nuisances." He eyed Kennon curiously. "How is it that you didn't stand on your professional rights?"

"I have my reasons—but they have nothing to do with medicine."

"Oh—I see. Ethical." The interne's voice was faintly sarcastic.

"Manners, Doctor—manners." Kennon's voice was gentle but the interne flushed a dull red.

"Sorry, sir."

"Don't mention it. It's normal for a graduate to confuse liberty with license." Kennon smiled. "Don't worry. I shan't report you."

"That's good of you, sir." Smalley's face registered relief. Demerits were difficult to erase—particularly ones of courtesy.

Kennon wondered if the young man would report himself. He doubted it. The interne didn't look the type—probably he was slated for some obscure job, like a general practitioner. He shrugged. It took all kinds to make a profession. Even the Smalleys had their place.

"That girl you brought in," Smalley said as they entered a white car emblazoned with the three crosses, red, blue, and green, that represented the three fields of medicine. "She's an interesting case. I've never seen space shock before. And the patient herself—one would hardly believe she was a Betan."

"She isn't," Kennon said.

"So?" Blond eyebrows rose in inverted U's of surprise. "But that's hardly possible. Our tests indicate——"

"Don't you think that this is a matter for Dr. Brainard?" Kennon said icily. "Protocol——"

"Of course. Stupid of me—but the case is so interesting. Half the center staff has seen her already. I wasn't proposing to discuss the case. It wouldn't be proper. Even though you are only a veterinarian——"

"Only?" Kennon's voice was hard. "I shouldn't have to remind you of this, *Mr.* Smalley—but I have been for the past two years on a world of bad manners. I expected better here at home."

Smalley flushed to the roots of his straw-colored hair. "Sorry, Doctor," he muttered. "I don't know what's the matter with me."

"I can tell you," Kennon said. "You've just graduated."

"How did you know?" Smalley said.

"I was a graduate once, myself—not too long ago."

"How long, sir?"

"Class of Eighty-seven."

"That's twelve years ago," Smalley said.

Kennon nodded. Ten years lost. Not bad—not bad at all. But Alexander could have done a lot in ten years.

"I meant no disrespect," Smalley said worriedly.

"I know it. But if you intend to practice on Beta, you'd better polish your professional manner. Now where I was, it didn't make much difference. Laymen often called me 'Doc.' "

Smalley was properly shocked. "I hope you didn't encourage them, sir."

"It was impossible to discourage them," Kennon said. "After all, when the man who hires you——"

"Oh—entrepreneurs," Smalley said in a tone that explained everything.

The car stopped in front of the Medical Center's staff entrance. "This way, sir," Smalley said. He led the way down a green-tiled corridor to an elevator—then down another corridor past a pair of soft-footed nurses who eyed them curiously—looking at Kennon's tunic and sandals with mild disapproval in their eyes. Smalley stopped and knocked softly on a closed door.

"Enter," said a pleasant baritone voice from the annunciator.

"Dr. Brainard—Dr. Kennon," Smalley said.

Kennon liked the man instantly. A plump, pink-cheeked man of middle age, with prematurely white hair, Dr. Will Brainard combined a fatherly appearance with an impression of quick intelligence. The fat that sheathed his stocky body had obviously not touched his mind. Brainard rose from the deep chair near the window where he had been sitting, knocked the ashes from his pipe, and bowed stiffly. His eyes —sharp points of blue in the smooth pinkness of his face— surveyed Kennon curiously.

"So you're the young man who takes untrained pregnant women for rides in old-fashioned spacers," he said. "Didn't you know what would happen?"

"I was in a hurry, Doctor," Kennon said.

"Obviously. Now tell me about it." Brainard looked at the eager-faced interne standing behind Kennon. "That will be all, Smalley," he said.

Kennon waited until the door closed. "Ordinarily," he said, "I'd never have done a thing like that, but there were some very pressing reasons. However, I should have given her an injection of Somnol before we started. I'm criminally liable. If anything happens to her——" His voice was tight with worry.

"You'd give *her* an injection?" Brainard said. "I hope you didn't mean that."

"But I did, sir. I've given thousands of Lani injections."

"What's a Lani?"

"She is, sir. The impression has been that her race isn't human."

"Nonsense—it's obvious she is."

"A Brotherhood Court of Inquiry didn't think so."

"Hmm. Is that so?"

"Yes, sir.—But before I go on, tell me, how is she?"

"Oh, she'll be fine. A little mental therapy and plenty of rest are all she needs. She's a remarkably healthy young woman. But this is beside the point. There are a number of unusual features about this case that need investigation." Brainard took a standard hospital form from his desk. "Mind if I ask you some questions, Doctor?"

"Not at all—but you are due for some unpleasant shocks as you go through that form."

"I believe I can survive them," Brainard said dryly.

"This is professional confidence—" Kennon began.

"Of course, of course," Brainard said impatiently. "Now let's get on with it."

"This is the most amazing tale I've ever heard," Brainard said slowly. "Are you certain you are telling the truth?"

Kennon grinned. "I don't blame you for not believing me—but the evidence is conclusive, and there is enough documentary evidence in the space ship—and in the fact of the ship itself to prove what I am saying. Laboratory tests here will establish the fact that Copper's child is also mine. And as for Flora, a Brotherhood Investigation Team can prove that part."

"That will be attended to," Brainard said grimly.

"But how did you deduce she wasn't from a Betan colony?" Kennon asked.

Brainard smiled. "That wasn't hard. Her sun tan and the condition of her feet proved she was a practicing nudist. No Betan girl ever practices nudism to my knowledge. Besides, the I.D. tattoo under her left arm and the V on her hip are no marks of our culture. Then there was another thing—the serological analysis revealed no gerontal antibodies. She had never received an injection of longevity compound in her life. This might occur, but it's highly improbable. The evidence indicates that she's extra-Betan."

Kennon nodded.

"But this business of her being fifteen years old! That's impossible. She has the development of a woman of twenty-five."

"Remember the Alpha V colony?" Kennon said.

"Of course—oh—I see! It could be something like that. Certainly—strong yellow G-type sun—an isolated colony serviced at twenty-year intervals—there was a marked physical precocity."

"And if this had been continued for several millennia?" Kennon asked.

"Hmm—I see. Yes, it's possible. On Alpha V the colonists grew from infancy to maturity in fifteen years."

"And wasn't Heaven one of our early colonies?"

"Yes—it was established after the Great Schism near the end of the First Millennium—when science and religion split irrevocably on this world. We packed the whole lot of them off to a world of their own where they could develop as they pleased. They called it Heaven—odd name for a fogworld—but there's no accounting for tastes." Brainard chuckled.

"I thought that was the case, but I couldn't remember. My ancient history is pretty weak."

"You should read more," Brainard said. "But as I see it —this girl is of Betan ancestry providing your theory and the facts coincide."

"Which could also explain why an outworld species of agerone would be toxic. They tried to prolong Lani life and met with failure. Our plants are mutant forms."

"Just as we are a mutant race," Brainard said, "or partly mutant." He sighed. "You have brought us a great deal of trouble, Kennon. You are bringing matters to a head. If our investigations prove your statements, we are morally bound to open the Lani question. And if those people are of Betan origin—that fellow Alexander will have plenty to answer for."

"I don't believe it is really his fault," Kennon said slowly. "I don't think he has ever known the truth."

"Why didn't you tell him?"

"The answer to that should be obvious. Even though I trusted him completely, I could never be sure. He has a Free Trader background and those people can't be trusted where money's concerned. The whole Kardonian culture is an outgrowth of Free Traderism: small business, independent corporation, linear trusts, and all the cutthroat competition such a culture would naturally have. It's a regular jungle of Free Enterprise. I couldn't predict *how* he would react. He could either act in a moral manner and make restitution, or he could quietly cut our throats and go on with his business."

"I see. The temptation to cut a throat might be overwhelming."

"They fight commercial wars," Kennon said.

"Disgusting—utterly uncivilized! Under the circumstances you had no other course. Still, they have no moral right to enslave human beings."

"There is always the element of doubt. Maybe they didn't know. After all, an impartial court declared the Lani alien—and the Betan mutation isn't known throughout the Brotherhood."

"One doesn't go around broadcasting data on the variations of one's germ plasm," Brainard said. "That's a private affair—a matter of personal privacy."

"And public safety?"

Brainard nodded. "We're no more courageous than any other civilization. We have no desire to borrow trouble. We are content to leave things alone."

"That's the trouble," Kennon said. "We're all content to leave things alone. If I hadn't found the spaceship I'd not have been able to lay aside my moral conditioning. And if I had not, Copper would not have become pregnant and forced me into these drastic actions. It's even possible that I would have done nothing." He grimaced. "And when I left Alexander's employment mnemonic erasure would have removed all memory of the Lani's human origin." He shrugged. "I still am not certain that it wouldn't have been the wiser course. Naturally, once I knew, I couldn't do anything else than what I did."

"Naturally," Brainard said. "Humanity reaches the heights when it faces questions of moral responsibility."

"To mankind," Kennon added heavily. "We have a convenient blind spot regarding our moral responsibility to other intelligent races."

"A harsh fact, but true—and who is to judge whether it is right or wrong? We achieved dominance of Earth by our moral responsibility to family, tribe, and nation—and we nearly exterminated ourselves when we forgot that this responsibility went beyond nations and embraced all mankind. We learned that after the Exodus. As for the other races—perhaps someday we will learn moral responsibility for all intelligence—but we are not ready for that yet. That's too big a mental hurdle." Brainard sighed. "We are what we are, and we change slowly. But we change."

"True enough," Kennon said. "But it's hard to be philosophical about it."

"You're young. Live a couple of centuries and you will understand patience."

Kennon smiled.

"You know," Brainard said thoughtfully, "you still have plenty of things to do."

"I know. I'll have to make a transcript of this discussion, have it witnessed, and make a sealed record. I have to arrange for the reposition of the evidence inside the Egg, and a complete recording of the Egg itself."

"And to be safe you'll need several facsimiles, properly attested. The arms of these outworld entrepreneurs are long, and unfortunately not all Betans are models of honesty."

"I'd better get started then."

"Let me help you," Brainard said. "I have a little influence in this area—and your cause interests me." He picked up the phone on his desk.

Kennon sighed. He had found an ally.

CHAPTER XIX

"What are you going to do with that girl?" Brainard asked.

"Formalize our mating as soon as she is able to get out of bed," Kennon replied.

"She is an ignorant, untrained savage!" Brainard protested. "You should hear the stories the nurses tell about her!"

Kennon chuckled. "You don't have to tell me about those. I've lived with Lani for two years. But she's not stupid."

"What are your plans?"

"After we establish her humanity legally," Kennon said, "I'm going to send her to school."

"For twenty years?"

"If necessary. But I don't think it will take that long. She has some schooling."

"But no training—and what of the Lani in the meantime?"

"I have plans for that. I'm going back to Kardon and give Alexander a chance to make restitution. I think he is an honorable man. Slavery may be as revolting to him as it is to any civilized human. He deserves a chance to rectify his grandfather's error."

"That is reasonable—and in the best traditions of the Brotherhood."

"Furthermore, it's practical," Kennon said. "Alexander is the only one fully qualified to handle the problems of enfranchisement. He's known the Lani all his life, and he is an executive type. A Brotherhood committee would probably botch the whole affair. What with colonial jurisdiction, territorial rights, and all the legal quibbling that committees love, the Lani would get a poor deal. And there's no reason to wreck the lives of a couple of hundred million Kardonians because the rightful owners of Kardon were illegally enslaved. That happened too long ago to have any practical meaning. There are other and better solutions."

"What?"

"How should I know?" Kennon asked. "But I'm sure Alexander will. That's his field."

"All you have to worry about is whether he'll co-operate," Brainard said.

"He'll co-operate once he knows the score," Kennon said confidently. "And he'll have to make some form of restitution. But it shouldn't involve Kardon. Actually the Lani were never in a position to develop that world. They'd probably have remained on Flora indefinitely. The old court records showed no tendency for their culture to expand. They were an inbred group, a static, balanced society in harmony with their environment. In nearly thirty-five hundred years their numbers increased only to a few thousand. Actually there is a good possibility that the race would ultimately have died out if Old Alexander hadn't enslaved them and instituted a controlled breeding program. There are more Lani alive today than there were at the height of their power. So in a way Old Alexander did them a favor. He kept their race alive. All we can expect is a fair and just settlement."

"But if Alexander doesn't co-operate?"

"That's where you come in. You'll be a watchdog. If you don't receive annual progress reports from me—and see or talk to me personally every second year, you are released from our bond and can do what you wish with the evidence I've accumulated."

"We'd better get this into Private Record," Brainard said. "We can transcribe an agreement and place it in the Public Repository."

"A good idea and we'd better waste no time. Alexander might still be looking for me—and if he is, it's merely a question of time before he catches up."

"Ten years have passed. It's doubtful. But we could keep you here at the Center."

Kennon shook his head. "Too dangerous. And besides it would compromise you. No—we'll get everything possible done to make the Lani's case airtight, and then I'll return to Kardon. It will put our case in a better light if it ever comes to trial, if I go back voluntarily. Anyway—I'm morally bound to return. Now let's make this record."

"It's your decision," Brainard said. "And it's your neck— but I must admit that I agree with you."

"I'll feel safer when we get the legal details clarified," Kennon said.

"And what of the girl?"

"Can you take care of her if I have to leave quickly?"

"Of course. I'll give her personal attention, and after she has her child I'll see that she is sent to you."

"That's decent of you, Doctor."

"It's my moral responsibility," Brainard said as he slipped a new tape into the recorder.

Copper responded quickly to rest and therapy. The space shock cleared up quickly. The gerontological treatments put her to bed again, but within a month she was completely normal, and her lifespan was now that of a normal human. She could look forward to some four hundred years with Kennon—and the prospect was not unpleasant. The Center fascinated her. Never before had she seen a hospital devoted to the care and treatment of humans. It was a far cry, in its polished steel and stone magnificence, from the tiny primitive structure over which Kennon had presided. Yet both places served the same purpose. Perhaps Kennon was right—that there was no difference between man and Lani. The idea was not nearly as unbelievable as it was at first.

"I never realized what it meant to be human," Copper said as she held Kennon's hand. "It is nice to feel important and to know that our child is a member of the race that rules the galaxy."

"So you're convinced?" Kennon chuckled.

"The serological identity—" she began.

"Hmm. You've been getting some education, I see."

"Well," Copper smiled, "I didn't think you wanted a stupid woman. I can read—and since you are around so seldom nowadays, there is little else to do. I've been reading history, medicine, and novels," she finished proudly.

"A fine catholic selection," Kennon said, "Now if you add

mathematics, sociology, and philosophy you'll have a well-rounded basic education."

"Dr. Brainard has been trying something he calls 'hypno.' He says it will help me learn faster. But I can't see that it's done much good."

"You won't until you need the information," Kennon said. "That technique is only good for implanting basic knowledge, and much of that will merely supplement or complete that which you already have. You won't be conscious of it."

"Oh—I think I see what you mean."

"Of course, you'll have to continue your formal education. There's a great deal for you to learn. It should keep you busy while I'm away."

"Away? Where are you going?"

"Back to Kardon."

"But you can't! Alexander will destroy you."

"I think not. After all, ten years have elapsed since we left there and he's had plenty of time to think. Douglas must have told him about us. I wouldn't be surprised if he has already done something about your people."

She shivered. "He might—but the question is what would he do? He could have killed them all!"

Kennon shook his head. "I don't think so. He never struck me as a mass murderer."

She shook her head. "You don't know the Alexanders like I do. I was raised by them. They're capable of anything. But what is this business of ten years? That's silly. I haven't had my child yet—and it doesn't take ten years of pregnancy to produce a baby."

"It's the difference between subjective and objective time," Kennon said. "We traveled here through hyperspace—low Cth—in an uncompensated ship, and there is little temporal flow in the levels below the blue."

"Oh—of course."

Kennon chuckled. "That would have been Greek to you a couple of weeks ago. See where that basic data fits?"

"But I've always known that."

"You just think you have. Search your memory and see if I'm not right."

Copper shook her head. "It's very strange," she said. "But that's not important. This idea of going back to Kardon, though—that's a different thing—that *is* important."

"I have to do it. Not only because it's a personal moral obligation but also because of the Lani. They must have their freedom."

"Providing there are any still alive."

140

"Stop being a calamity howler. Whatever Alexander may be, he's not a butcher. He even loved a Lani once. You told me so yourself. And he couldn't kill where he loved."

She nodded. "I suppose you're right, but I've never lost my fear of the Man Alexander. He held the power of life and death over me. But if you must go then I should go too. My obligation is greater than yours."

"Later," Kennon said. "You're not ready to return. It will be time enough after you have learned some civilized habits."

Copper's face lengthened. "You mean like wrapping myself in cloth like these people do?"

"That's part of it."

"Why can't they be sensible—or are they so ashamed of what the gods gave them that they must hide themselves?"

"No, it's not that. At least not exactly. It's custom. And you must learn to conform to customs—outwardly at least —no matter what you may really think."

"Isn't that a form of lying?" Copper asked.

"I suppose so."

"Isn't that strange. Your society exalts truth, honor, morality, and intelligence—yet you lie about your attitude."

"It's called diplomacy," Kennon said. "It's part of respect for others' attitudes and beliefs, a necessary part of human relationships."

"Then you'd be a nudist on Santos?"

"Of course—even though I think it isn't proper, I couldn't inflict my ideas and attitudes on the customs of an independent world."

"Oh—you think I'm doing that?"

"Yes—and it is a mark of barbarism."

"Sometimes you're not very nice," Copper said.

Kennon smiled wryly. "I suppose I'm not," he agreed.

"I'll try to be civilized," Copper said. "But if you go to Kardon—I'm going with you."

"Perhaps," Kennon said. "We'll see how things turn out."

"You don't want me to go with you?"

"To be honest—no," Kennon said. "You're safe here, and until your status is cleared by a Brotherhood court, I wouldn't care to place you in Alexander's hands. And clearing your status is going to take time."

"You mean that I am still his property?"

"Yes. But there is a legal doubt that will prevent him from exercising his claim as long as you stay on Beta. In the area where he has power, that doubt might not hold. So until your status is definitely proven to be human, you should not leave."

"And what happens if this court denies my claim?"

"Then we appeal to the Council. However, with the evidence we have, your claim cannot reasonably be denied. The only question is one of time. It may take years. Still, I don't think there is anything to worry about. I don't think Alexander will give us any trouble, but there's no sense in taking chances."

"You still think I'm a Lani," she said accusingly.

"I do not."

"Then you think that I'd obey Alexander, after what I did to Douglas."

"I can only repeat that Douglas isn't the Boss-man."

"I wish I knew what you *really* thought."

"That isn't hard. I think you should stay here until I get this business straightened out."

"That's all?" she asked suspiciously. "After all, I know I'm not very pretty now. And there's lots of Lani on Flora——"

"Oh, for Ochsner's sake! Do you think that I'm——" He paused, speechless. "Just what do you think I am?"

"You're a man. And that's the trouble."

Kennon chuckled. "So that's it! You don't trust me."

"I love you," Copper said.

"Sometimes I wonder why men ever finalize their status with women," Kennon murmured. "It does no good. It doesn't convince the woman. She's still fearful, jealous, and suspicious—always belittling her ability to hold what she has, always alert for competiton, clinging, holding, absorbing—when she should be working as part of a team."

"That's not true!"

"Then prove it."

"How—by staying here while you go to the end of the galaxy and play noble?"

"I'm only doing what I have to do."

"And so am I—and if you go I'm going with you."

Kennon shrugged. There was no sense arguing. The only thing to do was make his plans and leave quietly. If she was faced with an established fact, she might be more reasonable. He doubted it, but alone, she could do nothing—and Brainard would see that she was comfortable. The salvage money from the Egg would keep her from being a public charge. And he had more banked in Albertsville which he could send her once he got there. He'd start making plans to leave as soon as possible.

Copper looked up at him as he stood above her bed. Slowly she reached out and placed one slim hand in his. "I know what you are thinking," she said, "and—" her face twisted in a grimace of pain, and the hand in his clutched with convulsive strength at his fingers.

"What's the matter?" he said.

"Nothing—it's perfectly normal," she said. "I'm just going to give you a son. Now if you'd call for the doctor, perhaps we can get this over. That pain was only twenty minutes from the last. I think it's about time."

Kennon—who had attended several hundred Lani births and had developed a certain callousness about them—was suddenly frightened and helpless as he pushed the call button. He could feel the cold sweat form on his forehead. He had started this. It was his fault if anything went wrong. He wished that it was someone else rather than Copper who was going through this trial. He was nervous, unsure, and guilty. In a word, he felt like a man whose mate was giving birth to their first child.

"It's a boy," Dr. Brainard said. He smiled down at Kennon's haggard face.

"How is Copper?" Kennon asked.

"Fine—she's healthy as a horse."

Kennon winced at the cliché. It was so ancient that it had lost all meaning. Most Betans didn't know what a horse was, let alone whether it was healthy or not. From what Kennon could remember of veterinary history, the horse wasn't too healthy an animal. It was rather delicate, in fact.

"How is the child?" Kennon asked. It took a little courage to ask this question. The baby could be anything from normal to a monstrosity.

"Perfectly normal," Brainard said. "A true Betan type even down to the vestigial tail. We amputated that, of course."

"Thank Ochsner!" Kennon breathed. "I was afraid."

"Of course you were," Brainard said. "Do you want to see them now? When I left, Copper was asking for you."

Kennon sighed. Leaving, he realized, wasn't going to be as easy as he had thought.

"We'll have to keep them here for a couple of months," Brainard said. "We must take exhaustive tests if we expect the court to reverse its prior decision."

"I expected that," Kennon said. He shrugged. "It's probably best," he said. "Now show me where Copper is."

"She's back in the same room. You don't need a guide."

Kennon didn't. In fact, he behaved quite admirably.

CHAPTER XX

Longliners, Kennon reflected, didn't make Beta a port of call, and the Shortliner connections with other worlds were infrequent. Beta had done a good job separating from the rest of the Brotherhood. Too good.

The spaceline schedules showed only one departure in the next month, a Shortliner for Earth, and from Earth the road to Kardon was long and tortuous, involving a series of short jumps from world to world and a final medium-range hop from Halsey to Kardon. If everything went right and he made every connection he would be in Kardon four months after he left Beta. Kennon sighed as he left Travelers Aid. Morality was a heavy load to carry.

He walked slowly down the road from the spaceport toward the Co-operative where he had been staying. He had left Huntersville and Copper a week ago, after he had seen his child. His child! The thought of being a father was oddly dismaying. It distorted his sense of values. But one thing was certain. He was returning to Kardon, and Copper was not coming with him. She had a duty to their son—and he had a duty to his contract with Alexander, to the Lani on Flora, and to Copper—and none of these could be satisfied by further running. He had to return and settle the account.

A tall man in a conservative yellow-and-black suit was waiting patiently in front of his room. "My name is Richter," he said "—Art Richter. Are you Dr. Jac Kennon?"

"I could deny it, but I won't," Kennon said.

"Thank you, Doctor. It was just a formality anyway. You see, I know you by sight." He sighed. "One has to observe the formalities in this business." He drew a long white envelope from his tunic and handed it to Kennon. "Most of my subjects try to deny their identity," he said.

"It's a refreshing change to find an honest man." He bowed formally. "I really thought this would be harder, considering the charges against you." He bowed again and walked away.

"Now—what was that?" Kennon muttered as he opened

the envelope. The man Richter was undoubtedly a process server—but who had hired him? He unfolded the sheet and scanned the charges—coercion, larceny, livestock theft, and breach of contract. He shrugged. This was Alexander's work. What was the man thinking of? It was insanity to bring the Lani matter into open court. Hadn't Douglas told him what had happened? Couldn't Alexander guess that he had fled with Copper for a good reason—one that would stand up in court? Didn't he know about the spacer? Or had Douglas turned on his cousin? The pup had so many hates that it was possible. He was a natural troublemaker. Maybe Alexander didn't know. Maybe he was working in the dark. Kennon scanned the sheet quickly. Ah! here it was. Complaint— Mr. Alexander X. M. Alexander, Skyline Tower 1024, Beta City!

Alexander! Here on Beta! Kennon opened the door of his room, went straight to the phone beside the bed. He lifted the handset from its cradle and dialed the operator. "Get me Huntersville THU 2-1408. I want to speak to Dr. Brainard, Dr. Will Brainard. This is a priority call—my name is Kennon. Dr. Jac Kennon D.V.M. I'm in the registry—47M 26429 —yes—of course, and thank you." He waited a moment. "Hello—Dr. Brainard?—Kennon here. I've just had some news. Alexander's on Beta! Yes—he served me with a summons. Can you get a restraining order to prevent him from leaving? You can? Good! Here's his address." Kennon rattled off the location. "Yes—I'm taking the next airboat to Beta City. This should simplify things considerably.—Of course it should. He was a fool to have come here. Yes—I suppose you should tell Copper. Oh! She is? I'm sorry to hear that, but there's no reason for her to be angry. She should realize that I did this for her—not to make her miserable. Hmm.— She—she has? You think she should come with me?—Yes, I realize she can be a problem when she wants to be. All right then—tell her to pack a toothbrush and a few spare diapers. And see if you can get me a couple of tickets on the next flight to Beta City. I'll be over in a couple of hours and pick her up." He cradled the phone and dialed the operator again.

"I want the phone number of Skyline Tower 1024, Beta City, Mr. Alexander. Yes. I'll wait. This number is HUV 2-1278 and my name is Kennon, Dr. Jac Kennon 47M 26429. I called you before. No, I'm a transient. I can refer you to Dr. James Brainard, Huntersville Medical Center. Yes, I'll accept charges. Now will you give me that number? BCA 7-8941—thank you."

Kennon hung up, dialed the number, and waited.

"Hello," he said. "Mr. Alexander? This is Dr. Kennon.—Yes—I suppose you do, but I've been trying to get back to Kardon for the past month. You are? Well, that's your privilege, but I'd advise you to go easy until I see you. Naturally—I'm coming as soon as I can get there. We'll be seeing you tomorrow morning at the latest. We?—I'm bringing Copper, of course. I just wanted you to know."

Kennon wiped his forehead. Alexander sounded angry and dangerous. Ten years hadn't served to cool him off. What had happened on Kardon after he had left? Kennon shook his head. There was something here he didn't understand. The entrepreneur should have been covering his tracks, not threatening jail and disaccreditation. It was obvious that a personal visit was more necessary than he had thought.

Alexander was waiting. His eyebrows rose at the sight of Copper in formal Betan dress—and lifted a trifle more at the sight of the baby.

"What is this, Kennon?" he asked.

"Trouble," Kennon said. He took off his hat. "I came here to settle things before you took this case to court. You obviously do not understand what has happened. I suppose Douglas has double-crossed you. It would be characteristic of him. But before we go any further I think we should clear the air and let each other know where we stand. I don't want to make trouble if it's not necessary. You'll notice I'm not wearing a thought screen, so you'll be able to check everything I say, and know I'm telling the truth."

"It had better be good," Alexander said grimly. "I've been looking for you for ten years. I intend to throw the book at you."

"I don't know whether my reason is good or not. Technically I'm guilty of breach of contract and larceny of corporation property, but there are extenuating circumstances."

Alexander chuckled mirthlessly. "There are a few other charges. And quite probably I can think of more if you beat these. I'm going to make an example of you, Kennon. I'm going to drag you down and stamp on you. You're going to be a horrible example to all smart operators who think they can break contracts. It's taken a million credits and ten years' time to hunt you down, but it's going to be worth it."

"Copper's child is a boy," Kennon said mildly. "My son."

Alexander froze. "You can prove that?" he asked in a half-strangled voice.

Kennon nodded. "You see the extenuating circumstance?" he asked. "Suppression of human slavery!"

Alexander sat down. It was as though some unseen hand had pulled his legs from under him. "You believe it," he said. "—No—you've proved it! Why—why didn't you tell me? What sort of a man do you think I am?"

"I didn't know. I couldn't take the chance until Copper was protected. You see, sir, I love her."

"That isn't hard to do with Lani," Alexander said. He sank back in his chair, his face clouded, his expression troubled. It was obvious that the realization shocked him.

Kennon felt an odd sympathy for the entrepreneur. It wasn't a nice feeling, he suspected, to have the beliefs of a lifetime ripped apart and sent to the disposal chute.

"So the Lani are a human variant," Alexander said dully.

"The proof is here," Kennon said, "and the supporting evidence is conclusive."

"Which makes me—what? A murderer? A slaver? A tyrant?" Alexander clutched his head with lean-fingered hands. "What am I?"

"An innocent victim of circumstances," Kennon said. "You didn't know. None of us knew. And we still wouldn't know if the Lani weren't of Betan extraction." He grimaced painfully. "I've done some soul-searching myself, and it hasn't been a pleasant task."

"But it's nothing like mine," Alexander said in a low voice. "I suspected they were human when I was younger, but I denied my suspicions and accepted false facts instead of investigating."

"You would have found nothing."

"Unfortunately, that's not true. We discovered quite a bit from the experimental station you left us when you disappeared ten years ago. But we stopped when we found the age that was being indoctrinated with Lani tabus. We could have gone farther, but I didn't think it was necessary."

"Didn't Douglas tell you?" Kennon asked curiously. "I told him when I turned him loose."

"Douglas didn't tell anything except that you had somehow gotten a spaceship. I assumed it was one of those that were involved in that commercial raid a few decades ago, but I see it wasn't. No—I knew nothing about this development. And Douglas, I guess, wanted to keep it hidden. He gave your co-ordinates and ordered Mullins to launch a missile. But he apparently forgot to turn on his IFF. At any rate the missile lost you—but found Douglas. Douglas was still talking to Alexandria when it struck."

"He might have informed you," Kennon said. "If he had more time."

"I doubt it. He ordered the missile first. He was trying to destroy you before you could destroy Outworld Enterprises. His motives were selfish as usual." Alexander looked at Kennon with a haggard eye. "I owe you an apology," he said. "I've considered you responsible for Douglas's death for ten years. I've searched for you on a hundred worlds. My agents in every branch office have had standing orders to report any unusual arrivals. I have hunted you personally. I wanted to break you—I wanted to kill you."

"I couldn't help the delay," Kennon said. "The ship was old."

"I know. You've told me more than you think. I'm a telepath, you know."

"I've never forgotten it," Kennon said. "That was one of the principal reasons I came here. I wanted to see how you'd react when you learned the whole truth."

"And I suppose you gloat—no—you're not doing that. But you are right. I could have checked it further. But I didn't. Outworld Enterprises is far bigger than Flora—and I was busy. Galactic trade is a snake-pit. And, after all, there was Douglas's death—and the Family with their never-ending clamor for money and their threats when it didn't come promptly. I like being an entrepreneur, but until I made Outworld independent of Family control, I couldn't do anything except run the business to their wishes. Actually the island was only a small part of the corporation. I tried to run it as humanely as possible under the circumstances." He shuddered. "I don't think I was ever needlessly cruel."

"No," Kennon said, "you were indifferent."

"Which is just as bad," Alexander said.

"Well—what are you going to do about it?" Copper interjected. "You can beat yourself until you're blue, but that won't accomplish anything."

"What are *you* going to do?" Alexander countered. "You have the upper hand."

"Me?" Copper asked. "I have nothing. This is between you men." She lapsed into silence.

Alexander turned back to Kennon. "You have undoubtedly made some arrangements. You wouldn't come here—oh! I see. Congratulations. Handling the evidence that way was a wise course. You have my admiration. But then I should have known that I was not dealing with a fool." He smiled wryly. "Subconsciously I think I did know—but——"

"That's one consolation," Kennon grinned. "To be thought a rascal is bad enough, but to be considered a fool is intolerable."

"But your decision not to use the evidence unless you were forced to—that's poor business."

"But good morals," Kennon said. "Neither the Brotherhood nor I could settle this affair. It is a matter only you can handle. There is no sense in killing Outworld or throwing Kardon into centuries of litigation. The Lani never were numerous enough to lay claim to an entire world. I'll admit the club is there, but I'll never use it unless it's necessary."

"Why not?—it's sound business practice."

"I'm a professional—not a businessman. And besides, I haven't the moral right to return evil for good. You have not been a bad boss."

"Thanks," Alexander said glumly. "I've always considered myself civilized."

"I wouldn't go so far as to say that," Kennon said. "Honorable, yes—civilized, no. But none of us are really civilized."

"So?"

"We haven't changed much, despite our development. Perhaps we've varied a little physically—and we've learned to use new tools, but our minds are still the minds of barbarians—blood brothers against the enemy, and everything not of us is enemy. Savages—hiding under a thin veneer of superficial culture. Savages with spaceships and the atom." Kennon looked down at Copper. Apparently her thoughts were miles away in an introspective world that was all her own. She had said her piece and having done that was content to let the two men develop it. Kennon looked at her with odd respect. Alexander eyed her with a mildly startled expression on his lean face. And both men smiled, but the smiles were not amused.

"Judging from Copper," Alexander said, "I don't think we'll have to worry about how the Lani will turn out." He looked at Kennon with mild sympathy. "You are going to have quite a time with her," he said.

"I suppose so. I'll probably never know whether I'm guided or whether I'm doing the guiding. I've changed a lot of my opinions about Copper since the day I met her."

Copper looked up and smiled at them. It was an odd smile, hinting at secrets neither of them would ever know. Alexander chuckled. "It serves you right." He crossed his legs and looked up at Kennon standing before him. By some uncanny legerdemain he had gotten control of himself and the situation at the same time. Being telepathic was an unfair advantage, Kennon thought.

"You were equally unfair with your accusation," Alexander said. "Sure—humanity makes mistakes, and like this one they're sometimes brutal mistakes. But we are capable of atonement. Morally we have come a long way from the brutality of the Interregnum. I shouldn't have to use examples, but look at that"—he waved at the view wall at the panorama of gleaming fairy towers and greenery that made Beta City one of the most beautiful in the Brotherhood. "Don't tell me that five thousand years of peace and development haven't produced civilization. That's a concrete example out there."

"It isn't," Kennon said flatly. "Sure, it's pretty—clean—and beautifully designed for art and utility—but it isn't civilization. You're confusing technology with culture. You look at this and say, 'What a great civilization man has built,' when you really mean, 'What a great technology mankind has developed.' There's all the difference in the world. Technology is of the mind and hands. Civilization is of the spirit—and spiritually we are still in the Dark Ages.

"We conquer, kill, loot, and enslave. We establish standards to keep humanity a closed corporation, a special club in which men can live but aliens can't. We've made the standards for admission so rigid that we even enslave our own kind and call them animals. That's not civilization—that's savagery!

"For nearly five hundred years your family has run a slave pen. Your fortune is based upon it. And you have perpetuated this traffic in flesh on the specious reasoning that a court judgment of half a millennium ago is as good today as when it was handed down. Never once did anyone have the moral courage to re-examine that old decision. Never once did any human question the rightness of that decision. None of us are immune. We all based our conduct upon an antiquated law and searched no further. Everyone was happy with the status quo—or at least not so unhappy that they wanted to change it. Even I would have been content had it not been for Copper."

"Yet I do not feel that it was bad that I hired you," Alexander said. "Even though you have shown me that I am a slaver, and made me see faults I never knew I had." His face was drawn—harsh lines reached from nose to lips, from eyes to chin. Suddenly he looked old. "I can accept censure if censure is just. And this is just. No—I'm not